"Catriona, what were you going to say?"

Desire had stampeded her into a blind corner, and momentarily, she was unable to think of an appropriate question. "It wasn't anything important," she said.

She wished Cameron would touch her, hold her, kiss her. She wanted him. She shivered at the thought of his soft caress.

"You're all woman." His voice was rough with emotion. "So beautiful, so vibrant." His fingers lifted her hair and his mouth covered hers, kissing her so deeply that she was weightless, her consciousness soaring with his to the skies.

Reality was his gentleness as he feather-kissed her back to earth. She was content to let him hold her, aware of the new threshold they had reached, unsure of anything except her love and fierce need.

Rosalie Henaghan, born and raised in New Zealand, was inspired to write after interviewing Harlequin Romance author Essie Summers on the radio. Now Rosalie is the author of many books, whose unique quality stems from her use of events and elements from her own life to enhance her stories. She is convinced that a writer should examine her own background and then, as Essie told her, ''start writing!''

Books by Rosalie Henaghan

HARLEQUIN ROMANCE

FOR LOVE OR POWER
Rosalie Henaghan

Harlequin Books

TORONTO • NEW YORK • LONDON
AMSTERDAM • PARIS • SYDNEY • HAMBURG
STOCKHOLM • ATHENS • TOKYO • MILAN
MADRID • WARSAW • BUDAPEST • AUCKLAND

Original hardcover edition published in 1992
by Mills & Boon Limited

ISBN 0-373-03194-7

Harlequin Romance first edition May 1992

FOR LOVE OR POWER

CHAPTER ONE

'LOVE, fifteen!'

'Love, thirty!'

Love! The word twanged, irritating Catriona Macarthur as she tucked some black curls back under her head-band. Stooping, she snatched at the pristine white tennis ball and bounced it experimentally with her racquet, giving herself vital seconds to regain her concentration. At the opposite end of the court her younger brother Rory danced and swayed in cobra-readiness at his position well behind the line. She threw the ball up, then struck it with a hard, power-driven swing.

'Fault!'

Behind the sunglasses her blue eyes crinkled into a grim smile. She had made one mistake but she wasn't going to risk a second. The next time she fell in love she was going to make sure she was playing within the boundaries and able to control the game. Her thoughts pounded back and forth in time with the strokes. She had been stupid, of course; she should have realised a man like Ben Hamilton would be married. So much easy charm, so much fun! She frowned as she realised she had lost another two points. Ben was an excellent tennis player, too.

'Fault!' Her first serve just missed the line. She slowed and sent a serve which Rory slashed back, the ball touching the court, then fleeing past her outstretched racquet.

'Game to Rory.'

'What's wrong with you, Pusscat? First time you've ever given me an easy game!' Rory ran up to the net to collect the balls.

'You've improved, Rory.' Catriona managed a smile. 'You returned my serves. And that spin! It was great!'

'Do you think so?' Rory was eager for the praise. 'I've been working on it.'

'Too much so, at times,' Mrs Macarthur commented from the umpire's seat at the side of the grass tennis court which formed part of their large garden. 'University studies seem to be put aside too often. Rory, how you're going to pass your next exams... Your father won't put up with the few hours you do at the office forever.'

Rory grinned. 'Never mind, Mum, I'll join the sports set and play tennis with rich middle-aged women. If they're like you they'll be fit as fleas and good fun. Besides, Pusscat is doing us proud. She works hard enough with the family firm for the two of us! No wonder her tennis is going to the wall.'

'You haven't won the match yet! My concentration was abysmal!' Catriona laughed. Realising she didn't want Rory asking questions, she spoke again. 'Too much work in Wellington!'

'"Show me an office where the staff are slacking and I'll show you an office where the manager needs sacking!"' Rory quoted his father. He smiled at his sister. 'Dad's a workaholic! From the rumours I've heard, you're as bad. You know what the staff call you? Flower Power!'

Catriona smiled, her blue eyes a flash of light. 'There are also a few more doggerel appellations: "Snow White" has been almost forgotten. When I bought my Ferrari I heard "Wheel-Deal-Steel". I think I've lived down "the Daughter"!'

'Not all a garden full of daffodils and daisies,' Rory said with commiseration. 'And you want me to enter such a jungle, Mum?'

'Better Tarzan than a toy boy!' The sound of a car made her look towards the driveway. 'Match over by umpire's default. Your father's home early. I'll tell the housekeeper. Roddy, would you...?'

Catriona heard no more as she flung down her racquet and raced towards the car. Her father smiled his pleasure at seeing her and ordered the chauffeur to stop the saloon. Once out of the car, Sir James Macarthur enfolded his daughter in a bear-hug.

'Catriona, darling, it's good to have you home for a couple of days. You did a first-class piece of work on the Hemingway building.'

As he released her he gestured to the other side of the car where an equally tall man had left the vehicle and was watching them. 'I'd like you to meet Cameron McDougall, or, as you've probably heard of him, "the Black Scot," the Auckland manager.'

Steady, intelligent hazel eyes studied Catriona. She found herself remembering sunlit pools in the bush. Unexpected, delightful, they could also be dangerous and with surprising depths... The black hair was only one reason for his nickname. His dark business suit, pure wool finely woven, hand-finished, fitted him well, the excellent tailoring understating a lean, well-built physique. 'How do you do, Miss Macarthur?' There was just a lilt of Scotland in the deep voice. Catriona held out her hand and he shook it, his own warm. Faint scars and calluses and enlarged muscle told of hard work, but the nails were manicured neatly.

'Paeans of praise have been sung about your excellent work. It's a pleasure to meet you.' Catriona smiled, her admiration genuine.

'I want you two to get to know each other,' Sir James Macarthur commented. 'Business is easier if you're dealing with people you know. You should have met at Catriona's admission to the board of directors three months ago, but Cameron was overseas with a trade delegation, and at our last meeting Catriona was storm-bound on the Chatham Islands.' Sir James placed an arm around his daughter's shoulder. 'I told you to come home tonight, Catriona, so I could talk to you before tomorrow's board meeting. I've news for you, first as my daughter and then as a director of the company.'

'And it concerns Mr McDougall?' Catriona looked at the stranger. His quick flash of white teeth and the warmth in his eyes made him even more attractive.

'At tomorrow's board meeting I want Cameron nominated as chairman of the company.'

'Chairman! But Dad, that's your——'

'I'm retiring, Catriona.'

Shocked, she took a step back, her muscles stiffening while her startled blue eyes pleaded for an explanation.

'Perhaps I should have warned you earlier, but I like to have everything checked and in place before I announce my decisions. I promised your mother months ago that I'd take more time off, yet if I'm in the office I find it difficult to walk away. It's the chairman who holds the responsibility. I've decided I've had enough. The company's in excellent shape—we look set for another record year. Cameron is the man I've chosen to take us forward. As a member of the board and a key shareholder I'd like to know your vote is for Cameron tomorrow.'

Social graces came to Catriona's rescue. 'The special item on the agenda! Congratulations, Mr McDougall! My father could not have shown more approval of you.'

'I'm aware of that and it means a great deal.' Cameron's smile for the older man was natural and affectionate and Catriona knew a spurt of jealousy. The rapport between the two was evident. The arrival of her mother and brother resulted in more greetings and joyful explanations. Catriona noted that her mother welcomed the businessman as a cherished friend, while Rory, bouncing around Cameron, was like an eager puppy. It was obvious that both her mother and Rory had known of the impending decision and she felt hurt, acutely aware that, while she had been working in the Wellington branch office for a year, the family circle had widened to include Cameron McDougall.

As her parents entered the house Rory escorted Cameron to the guest flat. Left isolated, she returned to pick up her racquet and walked to the practice wall, her mind busy with the unexpected turn of events. Workwise it would not affect her immediately; she was occupied in her niche in Wellington and she had earned her place there. But long term? Somehow she had seen her father going on and on ... Rory and herself one day stepping in to assist him and later taking over as he had done from his father. Dully she realised it was a child's crayon picture which should have been screwed up and tossed out years before.

Rory had shown little inclination for the business, but he was young, just twenty-two, still finishing his commerce degree. He was so lovable, with his charm, understanding and open, joyful warmth. Given time, he would realise his shares in the business meant not only money

but responsibility. She slammed the tennis ball hard
against the wall.

Was the Scotsman an usurper, worming his way into
her father's consciousness? Did the quiet manner perhaps
hide devious ambition? Rory, at the age of twenty-four,
would inherit the largest shareholding, a family trust set
up by her grandfather and added to by her parents. At
the age of twenty her father and the trust lawyers had
given her control of her own share of the trust, but she
had completed her degree and was doing her postgraduate business studies. The trust retained Rory's
larger share, her father claiming it would be handed over
when Rory reached the stipulated age of twenty-four, or
earlier if he completed his degree. Had Cameron realised Rory would have his degree within months? Had
he reasoned that Rory, with a major shareholding, must
be a director? That, with experience as a director, Rory
would endanger his own plans? That Rory Macarthur
would become chairman of Macarthur's, like his father,
grandfather and great-grandfather, the founder?

She slashed at the tennis ball and it returned harder,
forcing her supple body to stretch. Surely her father had
hoped for the natural course of events? And wasn't her
father too young to think of retiring? He wasn't even
fifty. How could Cameron have convinced Sir James to
retire early? A wry smile flicked in Catriona's eyes. Her
father was a hard man to sell an idea to! The only person
who could handle Sir James with a smile was his wife—
and, of course, Rory. 'Ask and you shall receive' was a
phrase as right and natural as breathing to Rory, whether
he asked for himself, his sister or his friends. But she
couldn't see Rory asking his father to retire! The ball
bounced and Catriona missed the shot. Her father would
hate being retired—the notion was preposterous!

What would he do? Catriona rolled the tennis ball on her racquet as she glanced around, observing the immaculate green of the lawn, the artistry of the flowerbeds full of pink roses and dahlias contrasting with the silver dust leaves of cineraria, the blue delphiniums and the edging of blue lobelia. The garden? The last time her father had decided to do some gardening had been a disaster. He had thrown out as weeds the ranunculus and anemones in the woodland area, dug up the newly planted gladioli bed and pruned the shiro plum tree just after blossoming. The two part-time gardeners, proud of their prize-winning work, had threatened to leave if he ever did more than walk around the garden again. It had been years ago and Catriona had suspected her father had done it with deliberation, knowing that her mother would not ask him to take time off to assist in the future!

Realising Sir James loved his work, his wife had pursued her interest in horticulture, hybridising a forest of azaleas and rhododendrons and becoming a recognised authority. Catriona's eyes sparkled at the thought of her father following behind her mother in the garden like some devoted spaniel. The mental images were enough to make Catriona miss the shot and set up the next ball at a slower speed. Her mother would not be pleased at having her calm, well-ordered world disrupted by a hurricane-force like Sir James!

What else? Tennis? Sir James played regularly at home and on the staff courts. Read? An hour's reading would be enough. Balance sheets, on the other hand, he found riveting, and his expertise with figures was told and retold at morning-tea office breaks like Arthurian legends. Why hadn't her father mentioned retirement when he had visited her three weeks before? How and why had he given over the work he loved to Cameron McDougall?

Could it be possible he had been blackmailed into handing over control? But how? And why?

'Would you give me a game, Miss Macarthur?'

The Black Scot carried a racquet and was smiling, apparently relaxed. He had changed into an open-necked knit shirt, white with a blue motif, the same design on the pocket of his white shorts. The casual attire emphasised his tanned skin and the size and strength of his muscles.

'If you like, Mr McDougall.' She had nearly said 'No!' but realised it would make him aware of her antagonism. It would be better to judge once she had talked with her father; then she would study the facts. She caught the tennis ball against her racquet and led the way under the arch of budding red roses back to the court.

'Toss for service?'

'Heads.' Catriona noted he was not a man who gave away any advantage, even if he was playing a woman. She didn't know whether to be irritated by his lack of manners or to admit he was treating her with the dignity of being an equal player. He won the toss and she placed herself at the far rear of the court, assessing his ability from the first serve. Too fast, it overshot the mark by some distance and she moved up a little, guessing he would adjust his next ball.

'Fault!'

With his quick smile Rory had taken the umpire's chair and unintentionally honed the blade of Catriona's anger. Her nice-natured baby brother hadn't even realised Cameron had cost him the chairmanship. The tall, good-looking man at the other end of the court would find out she was not going to be a push-over. She was going to start by beating him at the game of tennis and finish by ousting him from the chairmanship!

The second ball sizzled down, but she lobbed a powerful shot back, then ran up to the net in time for his predictable return. She slammed the ball down and resisted the temptation of a smile at his surprise.

'Love, fifteen.'

His next serve appeared deceptively easy, but its spin forced her to cut it over the net, and he was ready, striking it with perfect timing just beyond her backhand reach.

'Fifteen all.'

'Fault!'

'Thirty, fifteen.'

Annoyed with the loss of advantage, she reassessed his play, watching the angle and the thrust of his racquet. She had to break his serve as she had to break him!

'Thirty all.'

'Forty, thirty.'

'Deuce.'

'Advantage server.'

'Deuce.'

The score bounced backwards and forwards and Catriona became aware that her parents had rejoined them, their applause for each good shot impartial. Their happiness made her idea of blackmail ludicrous. Their lack of favouritism annoyed her, and she slammed the ball and, with more luck than she deserved, it touched the inside of the boundary line.

'Game to Pusscat!' Rory crowed as she bent to pick up the tennis ball at her end. His endearing wink set her up as she began to serve. She would show the interloper how to win! Her serve had always been her best weapon!

'Fifteen, love.'

'Thirty, love.'

'Forty, love.'

She smiled, settling the racing nerves in the pit of her abdomen. Her services had each scored an ace. It was a surprise when he managed to control the ball and lob it back to her. Caught out, she failed to reach it before the second bounce.

'Forty, fifteen.'

'Forty, thirty.'

'Deuce.'

Remembering the advice of her last coach, she varied her serve. It caught him on the back foot and it was an easy return shot for her.

'Advantage server!'

'Game to Catriona!'

'Do you want to carry on?' Catriona asked, her blue eyes mock innocent. 'Are you a little tired, perhaps?'

'The game's woken me up. I'm in need of a little physical exercise after sitting so long,' he drawled. 'You're not a bad player, Miss Macarthur.'

The condescension of the man was a sandpaper rasp to her anger, but she retained her poise, acknowledging that he had repaid her remark. He wasn't going to be an easy enemy. As the third game went on the improvement in his play made it difficult to score each point. After long, wearing exchanges at deuce point the man's strength told; her right wrist, arm, shoulder and back ached from the dazing force of striking some of the balls, whereas Cameron McDougall seemed taller and tougher, leaner and harder. Determination and her fierce competitive spirit kept her fighting back until she won, but her honesty could not allow her to claim the point. 'I'm afraid we'll have to continue on another occasion,

Mr McDougall. We won't count the last game; the sun setting across the court makes it unfair.'

'Thank you for a great game, Miss Macarthur.'

'Well played, both of you.' Catriona's mother spoke up. 'Cameron, I can see you have had some coaching since your last visit. Congratulate him, Catriona; this man hadn't touched a racquet for years until the end of last season. He forced you to play to your top level!'

'Catriona always thrived on a challenge,' agreed her father.

'An inherited trait?' laughed Cameron as he looked from father to daughter. 'There's more to it than blue eyes!'

'Excuse me; I'm off to have my shower!' In no mood for after-game pleasantries, Catriona moved into the house through the french doors, clipping her racquet into its place along the side of the billiard-room. Walking along to the bedroom, she began to compile a mental dossier on Cameron McDougall. He played to the rules, but was that because, with Rory as umpire and her parents watching, he had decided he had too much to lose by cheating?

The game had told her more about Cameron. He had the grace of a natural athlete and, although his basic style was innate, it lacked the polish of consistent professional coaching. She would have guessed if she had not been told by her mother that his tuition had been recent, probably since he had discovered that in the Macarthur family the ability to play tennis was as necessary as the ability to make money! With his access to the executive personnel file he had almost certainly read their profiles and decided it was the way to charm and please. For all she knew the Scottish name and his black hair could be phoney; it was well known that her father was proud of being the great-grandson of pioneer emigrant Highlanders from Inverness. Reality forced her to remember the accent and that there was nothing false about the blue-black shadow around his shaven beardline. She smiled, imagining Cameron in a kilt. The Black Scot would look magnificent!

The shock of the shower made her realise the danger; she was beginning to like the man! Besides his obvious physical attraction and intelligence, was charm part of his weaponry, too? Had he sensed her antagonism and decided he would set aside time to allay her suspicions? The tennis game had had the appearance of a normal enough activity, yet was it all it seemed? She had beaten him so easily in the first two games; how had he developed the skill to force her back time and time again to deuce? A game of cat and mouse? But who was the mouse? And who the cat?

The blow-drier made swift work of her wet tangle of curls, then she applied her make-up with the speed of constant routine, finishing with cerise lipstick. It was the exact colour of the silk-and-linen-mix dress which she slipped over her body. With her height and dramatic winter colouring the result was sensational, but Catriona viewed herself critically in the mirror as she slipped into high-heeled cerise sandals. Her father was perceptive and she wanted to make sure he did not guess the heartache and broken dreams she had suffered in Wellington. She frowned, realising that she had hardly thought of Ben Hamilton since meeting the Black Scot. Cameron McDougall had thrust him out as though he were so much junk mail.

Glancing at her watch, she checked she had sufficient time for a long talk to her father before dinner. She had to try to understand, so she had a right to her questions. Surely he would have hoped the firm should stay under family control? Why did he want to retire? Had he considered all the implications? Why had he chosen Cameron as his replacement? There were other directors and company staff. Her own boss in Wellington was efficient, and had been with the company longer; the Dunedin manager was enthusiastic and ambitious; the Palmerston North office was run by one of the most able intellects in the company...

'Come in, Catriona.'

Her father had recognised her knock, and as she walked into his study she was dismayed to see Cameron at ease in the leather seat opposite her father. The Black Scot stood, and she registered the quick light in his hazel eyes as he took in her appearance. It was hooded almost immediately and she felt satisfaction at the knowledge that he found her attractive. Sir James had walked to the burr walnut cabinet, and handed her a glass.

'Champagne?' She raised her eyebrows.

'I think the occasion warrants it. I don't retire every day.'

'That's why I came to see you. I don't understand, Dad.'

'I'll leave you to talk.' Cameron began to rise, but her father, to Catriona's annoyance, waved him back to his seat.

'No, Cameron, you might as well listen in. Now, Catriona, you're wondering why I'm throwing in the towel?'

'Yes. I don't think you're making the right decision. You're fit, active, young, far too energetic to stop work. Just last year a week's holiday at the beach was your idea of boredom. Until you thought of building those waterfront apartments!'

'I've no intention of stopping work.'

Catriona frowned at the conundrum. Her father smiled. 'The country needs me. At least, that's what the government keeps telling me. To do my bit for society et cetera, et cetera!'

'You must be joking! You earned your knighthood years ago. Your donations and taxes look after half the country!'

Sir James looked towards Cameron. 'My daughter is inclined to exaggerate. It's her delightful sense of theatre!'

'I'm sure it is possible to give someone so beautiful a little leeway, Sir James.'

Catriona seethed at Cameron's fatuous comment, but her father laughed, clearly pleased.

'Yes, she is a beauty, my wild little red rose.'

'Not a briar——' Cameron eyed her '—a lovingly raised and nurtured cultured hybrid tea; a champion, surely?'

Catriona bit back her searing reply. If Cameron McDougall thought she was a rose then he would learn she had thorns. 'Dad, you're evading the question. What is the work the government has asked you to do?'

'They want me to set up a foundation with the aim of encouraging young people into sports and worthwhile activities. The figures on glue sniffing, drugs and alcohol-related problems are horrific. The tragedy of lack of self-esteem——'

'You, a Mr Goody Two Shoes! Dad, it's not your scene! The bureaucratic bungling, social humbug and form-filling would drive a saint to despair. And you're no saint!'

'I think I could help.'

'Dad, the best way you can help is to stay in your job and write a big cheque regularly.'

'I've taught you not to judge without the facts, Catriona. First from a business viewpoint, to put it simply, the chairman's job is too big. The company's growth-rate has been phenomenal, especially over the last ten years, and it's consistently demanding. It's damned hard work. You know the hours I put in when you and Rory were children. Then I could fly through it and look for more. Now I'm not finding enough hours in the day. I get tired.' He smiled, mocking his own words. 'Cameron and I have been working on reorganisation, which will shift a great deal of the load. It seems an ideal time for me to step down.'

'Tired? You?' Catriona's blue eyes widened. 'You've never been tired in your life, Dad. You always said you never knew the meaning of the word!' Astounded, she stopped speaking, and in the silence was horrified by her subsequent thoughts. 'Oh, my... Dad, you're not ill? You haven't suddenly developed heart trouble?' Agony at the thought brought swift tears to her eyes.

'Hey, you can cry at my funeral, not before! Where's that champagne? Do I look as if I'm about to start singing to harps? Look, Pusscat, I really want to do this work! I want to start over, to see if I can utilise some of my administrative expertise to help others. It's a new challenge, a new ball game.'

Catriona managed a watery smile. 'You, out of the chair, by choice? Dad, it takes a bit of getting used to the idea.'

'I agree, but it was a good, solid building supply and forestry company when I joined with my father, and we moved into property at just the right time. Like my father and grandfather, I'm not indispensable. Talents and times change. Of course, I'll keep my shares and my seat on the director's board, otherwise I might not be able to screw enough money out of the company for my foundation when Cameron starts his check of the exchequer!'

'Dad, I always thought Rory would replace you.'

'Rory? Hand him the company to run?'

'He'll be a major shareholder one day.'

'Catriona, you disappoint me. The family might own the major shareholding, but we are a public listing. Rory's my son, but I wouldn't trust him to run a file, let alone the company. The best thing I can do is hope that he doesn't get any control until he's matured. He's a lovable lad but he has no sense of responsibility. He's kept himself out of a director's chair! You earned yours; there was little nepotism in your promotion to Wellington. You're ready for your own area; the Hemingway deal proved your success, topping off eighteen months' profitable work. I'm very proud of you. I'm proud of Rory too, but that doesn't mean I can't see faults. You are individuals with your own goals, and Rory at the moment is more interested in young women and parties than he is in study or work.'

Catriona subsided into her chair as the silence in the room lengthened. Her father poured another glass of champagne and she saw his hand was not steady, Cameron's discreet movement of the crystal avoiding a spill.

'What would you have done in your father's place, Miss Macarthur?'

'You can stop calling me Miss Macarthur!' she snapped, aware she was taking her hurt at her father's reprimand out on the tall, quiet man. With an effort she controlled her resentment. 'I'll speak frankly. I hope my father's resignation is not accepted by the board tomorrow. If it is...' she looked straight at the interloper '...I will not be voting for you!'

CHAPTER TWO

'WITH your percentage of the company, you'd be over-ruled.' Cameron McDougall glanced at Catriona's father and gained his silent permission to proceed. 'But I'd like to start with unanimous support. Allow me to convince you I'm the logical choice.'

The self-assurance of the man nettled her.

'Tell us your pick, Catriona?' His cool question demanded an answer.

'The Palmerston North manager, Hemi Wilkie. He's been with the company nearly all his working life. He understands every facet: forestry, building supplies, construction and property. He's built what should be a minor office into one of the biggest in the country. Intelligent, articulate, he has the ability to take control, and the staff appreciate and trust him. With his own right to shares as a manager, he has quite a healthy investment in the company. He's also been a board member for several years.'

'But your father didn't select him. So there must be a reason.'

'He's turned down promotion before.' Catriona frowned, trying to recall the event.

'Family reasons. His wife's an invalid, and her family and his all live in the Manawatu. The head office is in Christchurch. Shifting to the south is not an option in his book. Otherwise he would have beaten me to the job.'

'You haven't got it yet,' Catriona reminded him. 'There are other directors.' Mentally she ranged through them. Several represented trust, welfare and insurance investments and they would not be willing to take the chairman's position. Others were long-term friends of her parents; two had their own companies. 'What about my boss in Wellington?'

'You can probably tell me more about him; do you see him managing the company?'

She stood up and paced the room. 'He's excellent at administration and handling the media. He always keeps the branch within budget, his integrity is unquestioned...' Loyalty stopped her.

'You need to be more ruthless. He lacks imagination, foresight. The second-in-command has enough for both, so they work well at a branch level. But two managing directors?' He was smiling.

'It could be an answer. Who said there had to be a boss in any case? What's wrong with all the board having a say?'

'Establish a committee? On what rules? Unanimous decisions only? They'd still be arguing whether or not to go ahead with the Macarthur Tower, built fifteen years ago. I approve of lateral thinking but in the end there has to be someone with a casting vote.' He poured another glass of champagne for her. 'I don't know if you've ever watched hens in a yard, Catriona. I remember it vividly. There is always an order of precedence, from the toughest, wily, largest bird down to the scrawniest weakling. With the order maintained, peace and harmony enable all to carry on, but put in a newcomer and the feathers fly. Feeding is forgotten until precedent is settled.'

'For a country boy you have a way with insults. I don't think the board would enjoy being compared to brainless chooks.'

'Did I say that?'

Catriona was irritated by his calm. 'I understand the importance of a smooth change-over. Otherwise the analysts will comment and the shares market will become nervous. Loss of investor confidence is one thing which tends to be almost self-defeating. We need our shares-market support to continue in order to reach the targets we've set. But I'm not convinced you have my father's abilities.'

'I'm not Sir James and never could be.'

His obvious respect for her father mitigated her anger. Mentally she ranged past the other staff directors and discarded them. 'Tell me why you should have the position.'

'Like your father, I enjoy a challenge. The work is exciting, demanding, but I find it rewarding. The results give me the lifestyle I want. My file will tell you I grew up in Inverness; my family live there still. My father and older brother run a small farm there and I've a younger sister, who is a doctor. I went to Edinburgh for my tertiary study, and I majored in engineering. I've also studied accountancy and law. After my masters degree I travelled and spent quite a lot of time on building projects, working my way around the world. New Zealand was a place where I felt at home. The degrees I possessed enabled me to get a job in the Palmerston North office under your respected Mr Wilkie. With his assistance and interest I leapfrogged my way from a casual to permanent senior management.'

'Yes, I remember reading his report on your promotion to second in charge, Auckland. He also rec-

ommended that you be made head there after the
manager retired. Let me think, it must have been about
three years ago.'

'Yes. Hemi Wilkie gave me the opportunity and I took
it. The Auckland office is now returning sixty-nine per
cent more profit.'

'You caused quite a storm with staff hiring and firing.'

'It was necessary. There had been quite a few castles
built up over the years, some of them guarded by middle-
management dragons basking in the sun of their early
achievements.'

Catriona noted his imagery; the Black Scot could
guard half a dozen castles, she decided. 'I know you
were responsible for setting up an office in Sydney, and
later one in Brisbane, and they have since become in-
dependent branches. How did you organise it?'

'I thought you'd completed a postgraduate course in
business studies?' His mouth twisted in deprecating
humour. 'Selective delegation. I followed Hemi's
example and checked the staff files. I know every
member of my staff and I try to understand their
problems as well as potential. Talent must be encouraged and rewarded. People react well to earned
praise.'

Catriona was aware of her father nodding approval
in the background. 'Rather basic psychology!' she said
with a waspish tone.

'It works.'

Again the simplicity of his answer almost defeated her.
'If you are approved as the next chairman of directors
what would be your strategy?'

'Much the same as your father's. Continued steady
expansion. At the moment we're planning offices in
Melbourne, Canberra, Perth and then Singapore. Your

father has mentioned some management changes but I'd
rather discuss them before the full board with all the
relevant details. The scheme is not quite ready.'

'Fair comment.' Catriona smoothed back a recalci-
trant curl as she realised she disliked to table a proposal
until she had analysed it and satisfied herself she knew
the facts, the difficulties and proposed solutions. But it
was also a smooth answer blocking her question. She
had no intention of letting Cameron McDougall off so
easily. 'Would you recommend further growth to the
Pacific seaboard?'

'It's tempting, but, at this stage, no. Too many
property-based companies have got themselves into
trouble by stretching their resources and investing
without sufficient study. Rather like planes flying without
checking the fuel. If we stay with the assets to share
backing we ensure consolidation. The credit lines are excellent, reflecting the financial institutions' trust. We
must keep our reputation.'

'I notice you are aiming for the larger centres. Tra-
ditionally our provincial centres have done well.'

'Yes, lower-section prices, better building staff, and
less transport costs have enabled us to offer prestige
blocks which have proved easy to sell or manage. Even
allowing for the lower rental, in several centres the capital
gain for our investment has worked out better than in
the metropolitan central business districts. I'm very aware
of the bread and butter background. But with the trend
today to head leasing I believe the major centres will
consistently give growth. That does not mean that if staff
see an opportunity in a smaller city they should not
follow it.' A trace of a smile touched his eyes. 'But you
don't need me to elaborate.'

She nodded and immediately a riot of curls broke away from the head-band. The loss of her professional image caused a glint in the hazel eyes of the man. She felt them look to her mouth and knew he was wondering about kissing her. Annoyed that the man could make her aware of his sexuality, she turned away on the excuse of re-filling her glass. As her father poured the champagne she was reassured by his smile, which told her he was enjoying the interview. Confidence regained, she faced Cameron again but he had altered position as though he had taken control.

'Can I say, Catriona, I was interested in the lease variation you worked out for the Hemingway building at the suburban mall? Following the lines you set could enable quite an upsurge in the suburban mall development.'

'You have seen the agreement?' Catriona was surprised.

'Your father asked my opinion; I couldn't fault it.'

His smile brightened the sunlit pools. She reacted with pleasure, aware that she had earned it by his approval of her work. He was seeing her as a colleague, a fellow director who was his equal. Her eyes met his and then looked to his mouth, and she realised that his lips were shaped with the sensuousness of a Canova sculpture. Seeing them lift into a knowing curve, she berated her instinct silently and moved her crystal glass up to the light as though the pause had been time to appreciate the sparkles of the champagne star. 'It needed doing. Before I make up my mind I'd like to see the records of the Auckland office. I'll go over them tonight.'

'I'll go over them with you.'

'That's not necessary. I learnt how to read a balance sheet almost as soon as I learnt my ABC.'

'You know how to access the records.' Her father spoke at last. 'Come on, admit it, Pusscat,' his hand rested approvingly on Cameron's shoulder, 'I picked the right one!' He heard his wife's voice. 'There's your mother, Catriona. I'll take her some champagne.'

There was silence in the room after he left. Catriona re-tied her hair, wondering when she had ever been so conscious of a man's attraction as she was of Cameron McDougall's. Even Ben had never caused her to be so alert, so aware of all the subtle sexual nuances. Yet she was behaving like a shrew!

'There's something else you'd like to know?' Cameron McDougall was sitting back in the leather chair, confident and relaxed. The knowlege prickled.

'Your personal life. You're thirty-one and, according to staff gossip, not married. Is there a reason?'

Fire flicked in his eyes. 'Do you mean am I gay? No.' He stood, the movement jagged as he turned away and looked out towards the garden. 'My wife died in Edinburgh six years ago.'

Catriona felt quick pity. 'I'm sorry. I didn't know.'

His broad back shut out her sympathy and curiosity. She could not cause him pain by asking insensitive questions. After a pause he faced Catriona, his features controlled, only the hint in his eyes showing his disturbance. 'Since then I've travelled for three years and then spent the last three years concentrating on my career. I haven't felt inclined to encourage any particular female into a permanent relationship.'

'A pity.'

'I know you approve of married men.'

The thrust was so perfectly targeted that the pain was in her face before she could control it. 'That's unfair.'

'You mean you can try being clever but I've got to stand and take it? I'll put up with it while you keep to business but not when you attack my personal life. Over that I give away no rights until I choose!'

Catriona wriggled her shoulders. 'Have I just been pecked into place?'

The anger in his eyes changed to reluctant appreciation. 'I doubt that's possible.' His left hand rubbed his chin, the long fingers scratching at a non-existent beard. 'I've heard quite a lot about you, but no one mentioned your humility.'

'That just shows how unobservant people are,' she retorted, her blue eyes smiling.

'I think I'll disagree with you on that point. Rory calls you Pusscat. Your mother always calls you Catriona. You're named for your great-grandmother, a woman from Inverness, I understand.'

'Yes; Rory is a family name too.'

'Rory remains Rory! But I heard your nickname at the office change from "Snow White" to the latest, "Tiger"! "Snow White" was a beautiful young woman who married her prince and lived happily ever after, definitely a fantasy. But "Tiger"? Fast, powerful, magnificent, dangerous and real!'

'My name starts with "Cat"!' she answered abruptly, not sure she liked his analogy.

'I think "Tigress" would be more appropriate!' He was silk-voiced. 'You're female, and the tigress is the more dangerous. But that's not enough...' he mused, considering her. 'You're more complex... "Titanium Tigress"!' He announced the name with triumph. 'Titanium is a hard metallic element we use in steel to withstand corrosion and to give strength without adding weight. Expensive, of course.'

'I prefer Catriona.'

'Even to the gentle, loving, domesticated Felis catus, Pusscat?'

The soft, sensuous burr in his voice undermined her decision to snap at his use of her pet name. 'I'm trying to remember when I first heard of the Black Scot. I think it was after you fired so many staff in Auckland.'

'Left as it was, the office would have started to run at a loss and everyone there would have lost their jobs. Sometimes it's necessary to make unpopular decisions.'

'I'll admit your name was said with fear and dislike, but now you're admired.' It was at that point Catriona realised her own feelings had etched a similar pattern. Shouldn't she be on her guard? Wasn't her father's interest in social work just too convenient? How much influence had Cameron McDougall carried?

Over the meal Catriona observed that Cameron was entertaining company and his affection for her parents and Rory seemed genuine, so she should not have been surprised when after dinner he accompanied Rory to visit friends. Her parents went out, and as she settled to the computer monitor she sighed, aware of her own loneliness. Life without Ben Hamilton was going to be rather desolate; she was lucky she enjoyed her work.

The Auckland records flicked into position as she inserted the floppy disks, and she decided to start some years earlier to build up her knowledge of the branch. She did an overall scan, then began finding that the pattern of growth had leapfrogged shortly after Cameron McDougall had been appointed second-in-command. The figures told the monthly results, and she accessed other files to lock into the Auckland area's complete records. Deliberately she searched back to the original ideas, all documented by Cameron to her father's guidelines. Tracking back the decisions to buy, sell, expand or lease, she tried to understand Cameron's mind.

It was after midnight when she leaned back from the screen and threw down the print-outs she had been working on. Her back ached; a ball of hot fluid seemed to have gathered at the stress-point at the base of her neck. Too tired to concentrate, she switched off the machine. A soak in the spa pool would revive her and drive away the intense fatigue while she studied the few remaining sheets. In her room, she stripped off, then pulled on her robe. Clutching the papers, she slip-slopped in fluffy backless slippers downstairs to the spa enclosed in one end of the large conservatory. With a loud bang the door slipped from her fingers as she gazed at the scene of Rory and Cameron with half a dozen girls cavorting in the spa.

'Come and join us, Pusscat!' Rory carolled. 'We're having a great time. Celebrating Cameron's promotion. Isn't that right, girls?'

Two squealed appreciatively, and one of the girls took advantage of the timing to climb upon Cameron's semi-recumbent form and possessively kiss him. As he lazily responded his hazel eyes flicked up to glance at Catriona as though to tell her he was more interested in kissing her. She felt suddenly savage.

'He hasn't got the job yet. Don't you think you're being a little premature?' Upset, she turned away, slamming the door shut to break the sound of their laughter.

Catriona looked round the oval directors' table. Apart from her mother, she was the only woman, and she made a mental note to query the point. The age of some directors troubled her; Cameron and she had proved that

younger directors could bring profits. She followed a
sharp discussion on the price of export lumber and decided to study the subject more closely. Her own interests
in the property and building section had given little time
to analyse the timber situation, so she abstained from
the vote. The rest of the meeting followed the agenda,
her father quickly reaching the general business special
item. When he announced his resignation, explaining his
wish to set up a young people's foundation, Catriona
saw that her fellow directors had all been informed; with
chagrin she realised that she had been the last to be told.

Hemi Wilkie gave a sincere, polished speech, re-
viewing her father's achievements and wishing him well
for his new position. There was no talk of refusing to
accept her father's resignation and, looking at her
parents' familiar faces, Catriona decided not to raise the
issue. The reading of the constitution of the company
relating to the selection of the chairman became a
comforting drone until the compulsory call for
nominations.

'Well, the firm has been Macarthur's with a Macarthur
at the head for more than seventy years,' began one of
the directors. 'Young Catriona has my vote any day. I've
known her since she was two weeks old and her grandfather proudly brought her along to the office. She's not
only beautiful, she's bright, and she has been working
with the company for some time. Recently she pulled
off one of the year's biggest and best contracts, and
before that she has proven her ability. It's not only her
father's blue eyes and her mother's charm she has inherited, Catriona has sagacity and judgement far beyond
her years. It gives me great pleasure to nominate Catriona
Macarthur.'

Startled, Catriona knew she had to act quickly. 'Mr Chairman, I would like to thank the director for his nomination. Unfortunately, I know that, although I've learnt a great deal, I'm not ready for the position. This company needs bold and wise direction from the chair, and a lot of our strength and credibility would disappear if the market realised, as it would, my lack of experience. As a shareholder I have the wisdom to decline in order to protect not only the company, but also,' she smiled, 'my own investment.'

Approving comment greeted the speech and she looked towards her father. He was smiling, pleased with her answer. His barely perceptible nod in Cameron's direction told her to continue. With steady gaze she looked round at the directors, but she had already agreed with her father's judgement. 'There are two obvious choices for the position. Hemi Wilkie has already refused for personal reasons,' she looked towards Hemi and received his affirmative nod, 'but fortunately Cameron McDougall is available. As a director, Mr McDougall has been responsible for some wise decisions, balancing entrepreneurial skill with sound economic and humane judgement. You are aware of his record in Auckland where major achievements have been recorded due to his insight, vigour, and staff training. Therefore, I wish to nominate Cameron McDougall as chairman.'

'It would give me great pleasure to second Cameron McDougall's nomination.' Hemi Wilkie spoke, and Catriona knew the rest was a formality. When the meeting closed Cameron McDougall had signed the chairman's contract Sir James had prepared.

After the meeting was a cocktail party for friends, the major shareholders and directors, arranged by her parents. Sir James made a brief but reassuring speech, introducing Cameron as the new chairman. The formalities over, Cameron walked straight to her.

'Thank you for the nomination; I did not expect it of you.'

'Because of the spa incident? You don't know me well, do you? I studied the figures and the background of some of your decisions. If you continue the same thorough assembly of facts before using your power I think you'll make the shareholders happy.'

'I sense the titanium tigress.' He looked at her, a frown replacing his smile. 'Something's wrong, isn't it? You approve of my business sense because you have taken the trouble to inform yourself. But you condemn me for what you think you know of my private life, Catriona.'

Startled by his perception, she admitted the truth. 'Yes. But, as you told me yesterday, that is not my concern.'

'Exactly!'

A group of shareholders approached to wish Cameron well, one elegant woman leaning forward to kiss him in a congratulatory manner. Catriona was aware of his mocking hazel glance in her direction before he responded by kissing the woman in return. Catriona realised he was daring her to remember the girl in the pool and make another judgement.

Disturbed, she moved away. Etiquette demanded she socialise, and it was something she usually enjoyed, re-newing previous contacts, making new ones and fre-quently learning of more than an opportunity or two which needed following up. The praise of several who followed the company's progress ameliorated her feelings, and she could see that the reaction to the day's news was favourable for her father, with recognition for his successor.

'You did well, Catriona.' Hemi Wilkie handed her a plate of artfully contrived canapés. 'Sir James is pleased.'

'Thank you, Hemi.' She would have liked to ask Hemi about his first meeting with Cameron but others were waiting to speak with them. A director representing a large investment group interrupted her thoughts.

'Like father, like daughter, Miss Macarthur! In less than five years' time you'll be a force to be reckoned with! When you ask next time for my vote you'll find me ready to listen!'

'I know you better! Unless my proposal is gilt-edged, your suport would be as dependable as cardboard after rain!' she chuckled. 'You're one of the hardest-headed accountants I know!' Catriona saw his glance slide to a newcomer who was walking unsteadily towards the boardroom suite. Disbelieving her eyes, Catriona excused herself and walked rapidly to meet Rory, her suspicions proved as he swayed, trying to put an arm around her shoulder. She grabbed his hand and turned him back before he passed the foyer glass doors.

'Hi, Pusscat. I hear you almost upset Papa's plans!' Rory announced, his grin wide, despite his bloodshot eyes with their dilated pupils. 'I'm still not even a director! The fat fees would have been handy. I'm always having to adjust the budget. Ridiculous! In two years' time I'll be the biggest shareholder in the company, thanks to Grandpapa's and the family trust. Sexist, eh, Pusscat? But I'll put it right; only fair you should have half...' He lurched towards a food trolley. 'I'll be worth megabucks. And here I am, working for...' he grinned '...peanuts!' He picked up a dish of them and proceeded to throw them up, trying to catch them in his mouth and missing each one by inches, his body unsteady.

Catriona shepherded him back towards the lift. 'And you'll be lucky to get that if Mum and Dad see you! Don't you dare move!' Propping him against the wall, she slid a chair under his hand. Rory being drunk was bad, but for him to be seen in such a state by the directors would be noted and remembered the next chance she had to raise his appointment. She sped back to the doorway, looking for help from a friend before her parents, hosting the buffet table, were aware of the situation. A pair of astute hazel eyes intercepted her gaze and she reluctantly nodded for his help.

Cameron excused himself from a group and walked towards her. Without speaking, she led the way into the foyer, where Rory was fumbling, mouth wide, trying to catch peanuts. Cringing inside, she noted Cameron's tightening of his lips as he understood.

'Rory, you're too late for the meeting but just in time to show me that new tennis racquet you were telling me about.' Cameron flung one strong arm around Rory and, with Catriona at the other side, he pushed the lift button.

'Congratulations, Cameron! Been celebrating! Feel lousy now, though.' He stumbled and would have fallen had not Cameron tightened his hold. The lift doors opened and Rory was guided in. Catriona tapped the button to close the door and descend to the basement level, where the family's spare car was parked.

'Cameron, you'd better go back. You'll be missed.'

'You need me,' Cameron said succinctly. 'Bring the car to us.'

There wasn't time to argue. Twenty minutes later Cameron accompanied her back to the lift, having left a sleeping Rory under the watchful eye of the housekeeper at home.

'Thank you. I'm very grateful.' Catriona was aware how stiff and inadequate the formal words sounded.

'I did it for your parents.'

'Rory was upset...' Catriona began.

'It's about time he stopped behaving like a mal-adjusted adolescent and grew up.'

'You can say that? After the way you encouraged him last night?'

'You couldn't resist that, could you?' He put out his hand and pressed the 'stop' button on the lift. 'Let's get this clear, right now. I went with Rory with the mis-guided idea that I could keep him from trouble. He's an overripe water-melon waiting to get squashed.'

She winced at his words. 'He's young and upset. I hadn't realised how much being a director would mean to him.'

'Stop making excuses for him. Rory wants the directorship for the money.'

'We need some youthful vigour and outlook on the board. There is a vacancy now.' She looked at Cameron, her blue eyes pleading.

'If you think I'd support Rory... That's it, isn't it, your price for my nomination? You want me to give Rory a director's chair.' His mouth twisted, giving away sup-pressed anger. 'And I'd heard you were one person who wouldn't ask for any favour.'

'I nominated you because you were the best one for the job,' she flashed, equally annoyed, 'but it wouldn't hurt to consider Rory. I think he needs responsibility.'

'Then he'd better earn it, like everybody else!'

'He should have his degree soon. If Dad gives him his holding then——'

'You heard what your father's opinion was last night. Rory will have to wait.'

'In two years Rory may be able to force you out.'

'In less than two years he might be dead.'

'Are you threatening Rory?'

His glance was cutting. 'Surely you can see he has a problem? You saw him; you saw his car in the basement.'

'Rory wouldn't have driven in that state——'

'No, of course not! He picked his car up and carried it to the garage just for fun.'

'One of his friends could have driven him. And he might have thought I was without a car. Stop trying to make out he's some kind of alcoholic monster. Or is he supposed to be on drugs?' Her tone was crisp and sarcastic.

He pushed the lift button, releasing it. 'There's no point in continuing this discussion until you acquaint yourself with the facts.'

Furious, Catriona found it difficult to face the guests and fellow directors and to appear calm and unruffled. Calling all her social skills into play, she moved from group to group, always avoiding Cameron. The occasional question about Rory she fielded with a degree of unease, part of her consciousness worrying over the possibility of truth in Cameron's charge. During the long weekend she would talk to Rory and see for herself. In the meantime her task was to be entertaining, informative and supportive of the new chairman. Time, usually so swift, dragged its hands round the clock. She wanted to go home to check Rory, but the success of the party told her it would go on for another hour, so she decided to phone home—the housekeeper would be discreet. There were telephones in the foyer but little guarantee of privacy; her father's suite was just along the corridor.

Stopping for an occasional chat, she worked her way towards the foyer and then slipped along to the heavy carved doors that shut off access to the chairman's suite. She smiled, remembering the ornate brass key her grandfather had given her so she could visit him at any time. His portrait hung just inside and it was seldom she passed the picture without a loving memory. If she had been the apple of her grandad's eye then he was the pineapple of hers. Rory had been named for him, but their paternal grandfather had died before her brother was old enough to remember him and his adventurous tales of the bush.

Pushing open the doors, she stopped, aghast at the orderly disorder. Three staff were packing books into boxes; on high scaffolding, five workmen were beginning to rip out the false-ceiling panels. Her father's desk was tipped ignominiously on its side and it was carted through the secretary's door. A smock-coated woman, head of the interior-design section, was standing next to Cameron.

'Put the original records in the safe storage of the basement,' Cameron directed his companion. 'The Macarthur portraits——' he gestured to two padded boxes '—can go there too...'

'Just a minute!' Catriona, blue eyes wide, face pale with anger, stepped forward, holding out a hand as though physically to stop the destructive action. She would never forgive Cameron! 'What is this? ''The king is dead! Long live the king!''?'

CHAPTER THREE

'CATRIONA! What are you——?'

'Doing here?' she interrupted. 'I think I could ask the same question. Except it is obvious.'

Smoothly Cameron walked towards Catriona. 'You'll get your beautiful face and suit dusty if you stay here, lass. Allow me to escort you back to the party.' He offered his arm as if they were walking into dinner. *Sotto voce* he murmured, 'If you don't want to make an even bigger fool of yourself you'll do as I say.'

'And allow you to shove Grandad and his father down into the basement?'

'Their pictures will be safe; the lack of light and the cooler temperature will keep——'

'They are not going in any fusty old cupboard in the basement!' She stormed across the room to where two men were lifting one of the boxes. 'Take the portraits to my father's house with the rest of his personal belongings.'

'Ignore Miss Macarthur,' Cameron signalled to the men. 'The portraits belong to the company, and as they're valuable artworks I'm afraid I cannot allow them to leave this building.'

'You insensitive...' Catriona found her words silenced by the black depth in Cameron's eyes.

'You and I need to have a little chat. In private. Now!'

She winced under the whip of his words but she was not ready to declare defeat. Catching amused glances from the still workers, Catriona realised her slanging-match with the new chairman was very public. Cameron's stare set the workers rushing back into action like battery-powered toys. Catriona led the way to the lift. Without speaking, she tapped the level for the staff lounge three floors down. Indignation, hurt and anger clasped in her tight hands, she kept silent as the red-lit numerals indicated their descent. When the lift opened she walked to the empty room, snapping on lights as she went. Cameron shut the door then gestured her to a chair, but she shook her head; she was in no mood to fall into a submissive trap. Irritating her with his confidence, Cameron leaned against a pillar, one leg casually crossing the other.

'Catriona, as a director you have specific duties dependent on your judgement. Aside from that, there are some other classic virtues I regard as essential: cooperation, respect and loyalty for the chair in public.'

'Respect? Loyalty?' The words were kerosene-soaked chips on the smouldering fire of her anger. 'And you demolishing my father's office within an hour or two of becoming chairman! That's respect? Throwing the founders' portraits into the basement! Is that loyalty? Don't you dare lecture me!'

He straightened, planting both feet, leaning forward to make his attitude clear. 'I'm not lecturing, I'm informing you. In public I expect total support. If you don't know the facts then don't make assumptions. The incident just now was deplorable. There were several staff in that room and most will gossip about your performance. If you'd stood and shouted it at a Press conference you'd hardly have spread the word more effectively that you act without thought. They will also believe that you don't give a damn about my authority as chairman. That I will not tolerate!'

'You talk about me acting without thought!' She heard the rage rise in her voice and with an effort she controlled her fury. 'I may be a director but that has nothing to do with my feelings as a daughter for the untimely destruction of my father's office.' She was crisp and hard, determinedly righteous. 'And the staff there knew exactly how and why I felt so strongly about it. You couldn't even wait one day before crudely stamping my father's work in his face. And you pretended to admire him! How's he going to feel when he finds out? As for respect and authority,' her blue eyes glinted fiercely, 'it's not given, it's earned!'

'In a few moments you'll accompany me back to the office and you will help me approve the decorating scheme you interrupted.'

It was a declaration of power, but she would not allow him to intimidate her.

'Do I look as if I'm playing games?'

His voice was deceptively soft. Again Catriona remembered the dark pools of the forest, their depths and their black danger. Uneasy, she moved away to the window. Could she be wrong? And what had he meant about making assumptions?

'You disappoint me, Catriona. I thought you were a woman who combined intelligence with beauty. Like so many beautiful people, you can't get past the first letter in the word "intelligence".'

'If you're resorting to personal insults then I don't have to listen!' She swept towards the door but he moved to stop her.

'Yes, you do! You have been so busy accusing me that you haven't once asked me to explain.'

'Explain what? That you couldn't wait to insult my father——?'

'Sit down and shut up!' he roared.

Her wide-eyed look as she sat in the nearest chair and his own recognition of his loss of control sent him striding across the room, thrusting his left hand through his dark hair in a gesture of raging frustration, his right hand shoved into his pocket as if to confine its movement. After gazing through the window at the cityscape for a full minute he returned.

'Catriona, I'm sorry.' He dropped beside her so that he was on her white-faced level. 'I've always abhorred creatures who rant and rave at others.' He looked at her, and the hazel eyes held wry honesty. 'The last time I lost my temper was years ago.'

They were quiet, each lost in their own thoughts. From the corridor came the faint noise of a vacuum cleaner and the indistinct voices of two cleaners. Below, the traffic sounds formed a murmur like a distant river. The ticking of the wall clock was a loud distraction. Catriona realised she had never heard it before. Always the staff-room had been full of people and their movement, the sounds of chatter, music and the clatter of teacups and coffee-cups.

'I seem to have been fighting you since we met,' she conceded, 'and I hate to admit it but, thinking back just now, I didn't give you a chance to give me an explanation about the office...' With a trace of her former spirit she spoke firmly. 'If there is one!'

'Dare I say that I didn't know anything about it until ten minutes before you walked in? Yes, you might well look puzzled.' His mouth lifted on one side in a twisted half-smile. 'Sir James organised it. A surprise for me. But work couldn't be started until my appointment, and he wants it finished over the weekend. He had the decorator standing by with sketches and asked me to check which I would like. I'd just finished deciding when I noticed that the portraits and the records were still in the room. That was when you walked in.'

'Dad organised it...a surprise!' she gasped. 'I'm sorry!' Catriona's apology was mingled with relief. 'I was so shocked...'

'A tigress isn't noted for asking questions before she leaps in defence of her family.' Cameron smiled and reached for her, pulling her upright as he stood. The movement brought them together. They stopped, still, looking at each other, aware of having crossed the other's space. She was conscious of Cameron's physical appeal, his magnetism attracting her, his eyes intent and her own sudden tumult of sensuality. Unwilling to move when she felt Cameron brush back the tangle of curling black hair by her cheek, she was tantalised by the stroking of his fingertips on her face as he lifted back the disturbed curls. His hands explored the outline of her face, tracing it with exquisite skill until his fingers curved behind her ears, his touch setting sweet, pleasurable sensations jangling through her body. Still looking into his eyes, she knew what he was saying, that he wanted to kiss her...that he wanted it to be special...that he found her beautiful...that he was sexually attracted to her.

She could have looked down and looked away, denying their silent communication, but she was just as attracted by the tall dark man and the sensitivity he showed. Lifting her arms to encircle him, she was aware of him bending his head, his dark hair gleaming, and she closed her eyes, her lashes brushing against his cheek. His lips touched and retouched, then settled, warm and firm, searching, discovering and claiming her flare of response. She felt him deepen the kiss, knew his hunger and demand. His lips moved to the tip of her right earlobe, wrenching even more response before he returned to the soft fullness of her lips.

'You have the most enchanting, kissable mouth,' he muttered as he released her, sense shattering moments later. 'I've been wanting to kiss you...' His arms tightened, rustling the silk of her blouse. Catriona nestled against him, enjoying the intimacy, her eyes content only to see the fine wool weave of his dark suit, the newness of his white cotton shirt, and the discreet silk tie. Definitely power-dressing, she acknowledged, and wished that he were wearing his casual tennis gear so that she could more readily feel his healthy, lithe body close to hers. She reached up and kissed him just below his ear and the subtle mix of his cologne and his warmth teased her sense of smell.

Her thoughts came and went, a merry-go-round spinning too fast. She was supposed to be in love with Ben Hamilton—what was she doing kissing Cameron? And in the middle of the boardroom party! Minutes before she had been in a fury with him. Yet she had responded to the look of recognition of attraction between them; she had wanted him to kiss her and he had read the desire in her eyes as easily as she had read the passion in his. The kiss had been natural, right and wonderful. She felt at home in his arms, complete with him. Guilt made her start, and Cameron brushed her mouth with the swift flicker of a bird's wing in flight.

'I know, Snow White must return to the castle.' He kept her close as though unwilling to break the spell. 'A great pity I'm not Prince Charming!'

She looked at him, wondering why he had declared himself ineligible, then remembered his wife. Her death must have scarred, and Cameron would have been only twenty-five. How long had they been married? What had happened?

'You look entrancing, but, unless you want everyone in the room to know, maybe you'd better rearrange your hair.' His tone was dry. 'One of the chairman's duties is not to encourage wild speculation!'

His reminder prompted her to look round and locate the bag she had dropped on a chair. One glance in the wall mirror told her it would be better to brush and re-tie her hair—her curls were an abandoned riot. Two minutes later she had disciplined it to a satisfactory state, and she tied it firmly. Only then did she realise Cameron had been observing her actions.

'Your hair!' he mourned. 'Loose, it's so beautiful, a riot of curls to entrance a man.'

'It was the wicked witch who made spells.'

'But you're Snow White, the fairest in the land!' He had come to stand behind her, checking over her shoulder in the mirror for lipstick giveaways and make-up marks on his suit before he began knotting and straightening his tie. Catriona reapplied colour to her lips.

'Now we know why we've been so antagonistic. Sexual attraction playing tricks.' His eyes in the mirror were rueful. 'Friends, yes?'

She remembered the portraits and eased away. 'So long as you don't banish Grandad to the basement.'

'It's temporary. The safest place while workers are ripping down the ceiling and painting et cetera. And the basement storage area has controlled cool temperature and low light.' He lifted one hand in a Boy Scout salute. 'I promise your venerable ancestors will be restorted to their dignity on Monday or Tuesday when any danger has been removed. All right?'

'Yes, of course. Where will you put them?'

'The decorator and your father suggested the
boardroom. It's hardly used and the air temperature and
light can be separately controlled. They are too valuable
to be in the heat of the main offices. The surface on the
earlier one is beginning to craze. I mean to get an art
restorer to give me an opinion.' He smiled, looking at
her, and stroked her jawline with his right forefinger.
'There's a definite physical family link in the blue eyes,
black hair and the strong jaw. It could make for
difficulties!'

'Me? Difficult?' Catriona's blue eyes widened in mock
astonishment. 'Not when I'm kept informed!'

'Exactly! So you'd better come along with me and
have a look at the decorator's plans.'

'I will,' she laughed, recalling his earlier order, 'purely
in the interests of the company.'

They walked back to the lift and then went to the
chairman's office. Catriona, studying the partially exposed wooden barrel-vault ceiling, felt the tug of
memory. 'I'd forgotten it was there,' she admitted. 'It
was made from some of the first trees planted by Great-
Grandfather Macarthur. This building was Grandad's
biggest and best.'

'A couple of weeks back your mother mentioned the
ceiling; she didn't approve of the decorator's ''modern-
ising'' it years ago. I guess your parents were trying to
find out my views then. The ceiling's a work of a
craftsman; I'm going to enjoy it.'

He turned to ask the decorator to show Catriona the
design he had selected. The sketch took her only a
moment to assess. 'It's very good; light and airy and
comfortable to work in for long periods. Accenting the
window shapes and the plaster frieze, plus the resto-
ration of the original ceiling, emphasises the traditions,

subtly keeping the image of the grand old company as being solid and substantial. Yet everything is there for modern business functions.' She handed back the design to the decorator. 'I'll look forward to seeing the refit completed; you always manage to combine artistry with efficiency.'

'Thank you; did you want to check the basement storage? I haven't locked it yet.'

'A good idea.' Cameron held out his hand for the key.

The decorator removed a bunch of keys from her pocket and, selecting one, handed it to Cameron. 'Remember the alarm.'

'Yes! I'll return the store key to Security. Thank you for your assistance.'

Catriona said goodnight to the staff, and the grins which answered hers told her the gossip about her fight with Cameron, although not forgotten, would be down-played by their amicable reappearance. As they walked towards the doors Catriona glanced at her watch. 'We can check the paintings later. Most of the guests should be ready to say goodbye.'

'You're right.'

At his words her eyes sparkled and her lips curved to reveal perfect white teeth.

'What a lovely, self-righteous smile!' he teased.

'I'm not a woman who appreciates flattery.'

'Then you're the first I've met.' His quick smile darted along his face into his eyes. 'Perhaps it's because you're such a beauty.'

'Indubitably!' she chuckled as he opened the heavy doors. The blinding light of photographers' flashes caught them unawares. She stumbled against Cameron and he steadied her, turning his back on the cameramen until he was sure she was ready. It also gave her time to

see the sign of apprehension on his face and she realised
he was afraid they would demand policies and strategy,
and he wasn't one to give a flip answer. 'It's OK,' she
murmured. 'Smile and promise them a media conference on Monday.'

The press of thanks on her arm was instant acknowl-
edgement. As he faced the reporters he was smiling,
urbane. 'Good evening, everyone. Most of you will have
met Miss Catriona Macarthur, a director, before. I'm
Cameron McDougall, and I hope to meet you at the
media breakfast to which you are invited on Monday
morning at seven-thirty, here in the boardroom suite.
Thank you for showing such interest in the grand old
company.'

Apparently relaxed, they walked past the security
guard holding the boardroom doors open for them. Only
the tension in Cameron's walk made her aware of his
underlying feelings, and she felt almost protective, surprised by his vulnerability.

'Every bit the chairman,' she smiled, 'and better
looking than the past one too!' She wrinkled her nose
and cheeks in an affectionate grin at her father, who met
them.

'I'm glad you and Cameron have settled your spat.'

'Dad, your spies don't miss a trick!'

'Where Rory's concerned they do! I haven't seen him!'

Reminded, Catriona felt regret that she had forgotten
all about her intention to ring home. 'He was here earlier,
briefly.' Her voice was over-bright, like the jagged edges
of a broken bottle. She had always found it difficult to
tell even grey lies.

'He had to leave almost immediately.' Cameron de-
flected her father's enquiry. 'Wished me well, et cetera.'

'Of course! I'd overlooked that he had to attend the extra tuition for his varsity exams; he's probably there.' Satisfied, he gestured towards the doors. 'Cameron, I'm afraid the news came out sooner than we'd estimated. The media gained entry when the workmen left the main doors open. I hope it wasn't too unnerving.'

'No problem, thanks to your daughter's prompting. A Press breakfast at seven-thirty on Monday.'

'Starting early! I'll be there to introduce you; then I'll bow out. Have a word with my secretary—she'll make the arrangements.'

They were at the end of the farewell line and Catriona found herself alongside her parents and Cameron, saying goodbye to the guests. Finally the room contained only the directors and their partners, and Sir James gave concise instructions for the transport waiting to take them to the Macarthur residence for the formal dinner her parents always hosted. Once home, Catriona slipped out of the main lounge to run upstairs to Rory's bedroom.

'Hi, Pusscat! I feel ghastly!' Rory rolled over on the bed and eyed her. 'I know! Disgrace to the family,' he groaned. 'Dad's big day! Don't you lecture me too!'

'Listen, Dad and Mum know you were at the cocktail party briefly but they think you went off for extra study.'

'I forgot! The Friday tuition session! Lousy time at any rate.' He checked the bedside clock-radio. 'I won't be due home for another half-hour.'

The housekeeper had left the coffee machine full on his table, and Catriona poured him a mug. 'Drink! Get yourself showered.' She went to his dressing-room and began laying out his evening attire.

'Bless you, Pusscat! Did you bring me home?'

'Cameron helped. You flaked out in the car.'

'Cameron?' He pulled a face as he drank some coffee.

'I'd better get downstairs.' Catriona blew him a kiss. 'See you soon.'

The dining-room was to the left of the main lounge, and Catriona swiftly changed a couple of the place-names so that she could be near Rory to protect him. Her mother would note the change of her seating arrangement, but, presented with a *fait accompli*, she would preside unruffled. Leaving the room, Catriona went into the garden and walked along the path to the main lounge. Cameron was standing by the garden doors talking to a small group. He glanced across at her as if he had felt her gaze. She saw him excuse himself and a minute later he was beside her.

'Come for a walk, Catriona. Let's inspect your mother's roses for aphids.'

'Don't let my mother hear you use such language!'

Laughing, they sauntered along beside the dahlia- and rose-beds, passing the tennis courts and the tall pillars laden with early flowering climbing roses, then they followed the neat path leading to the rockery overlooking the water garden, its stream rushed with buds of purple iris.

Cameron pointed to a seat placed under the branches of a kowhai tree. 'This has to be one of the most beautiful places on earth. To share it with you...'

A thrush burst into a love-song, finishing the tender compliment. The sight of the myriad colours and floral scents and the ecstatic bird call were enhanced because Cameron was beside her.

'The thrush is over there, by the maple. Look at him; you'd think he'd split his feathered chest—he's singing with all his energy! Can you see the female?'

'On the other branch.' Catriona pointed. 'See, slightly lower; she's making out she's unimpressed, but she's listening.'

'How do you know?' He reached for her right hand and kissed the tip of her longest finger.

'Female intuition!'

The interruption of another male thrush caused a loud flurry of song, and when the newcomer did not recognise the territorial signal the first thrush flew closer, placing himself between the newcomer and the female. The little pantomime was over suddenly when Rory walked along by the stream, scaring all three birds into flight.

'Indulging in bird-watching?' Rory jumped the stream, then paused, holding his head in mock agony. 'Be careful, Cameron, bird-watching can be a dangerous hobby.' He climbed the lawn to sit down beside them. 'Mum was asking for you, Pusscat.'

'I'd better go.' Catriona left reluctantly. She had enjoyed being with Cameron; the charm of watching the birds with him had been a simple pleasure and it had revealed his gentleness and appreciation of nature. At the top of the path she glanced back, but Cameron was speaking to Rory and, from Rory's expression, the talk was not pleasant. All her protective instinct was aroused but then she heard Rory's laugh and decided she must have been mistaken—no one would be able to lecture Rory!

On looking around she saw her mother escorting a group back towards the house after inspecting the garden. To intercept them Catriona crossed the little bridge and waited for them to approach. She was puzzled when her mother did not assign her a task but gathered her along as though adding another flower to her bouquet. Rory would not have sent her on a goose-chase, or would he? But why? Something to do with Cameron? Had Rory been so ashamed that he wanted to apologise alone to Cameron?

The ringing of the dinner gong summoned everyone to the dining-room, and Catriona, placed almost opposite her brother, was pleased to observe that Rory, although more quiet than usual, seemed to make an effort to please his table companions, his natural charm reasserting itself as the courses passed. His wine glass, she had noted, was filled with grape juice and, apart from a moue at first taste, he had not altered his choice. Catriona was relieved. If Rory had become too fond of alcohol he would have taken advantage of the fine wines her father and mother supplied for the occasion. Her own dinner partner was Hemi Wilkie, a witty raconteur; she had done herself a favour when she had switched seats! Once or twice she glanced towards the head of the table, where Cameron was on her father's right, but each time he was engrossed in conversation. He seemed to be enjoying himself, though when she succeeded in meeting his glance and he toasted her with his eyes she felt the sweet warmth quicken in her body.

The dinner and socialising over, the guests were driven to their hotel or the airport. Rory excused himself, leaving Catriona with Cameron and her parents. As Cameron was thanking them he slipped his hand in his pocket and took out a key. His instinctive reaction of guilt made her chuckle.

'I'm sorry, you'll have to excuse me, too. I've forgotten to check and lock the portraits and records!' Cameron looked at her. 'Catriona, you were concerned about them earlier. Would you like to come with me and see for yourself?'

'I'll get my jacket.'

She ran upstairs, her heart racing too, the prospect of a few moments alone with Cameron flooding her with joy. It was like being a child and waking to a Christmas morning!

'Let's walk! It's quite mild,' Cameron suggested when she rejoined him, 'very romantic.'

She noted the Scots burr in his voice—it became much more obvious when his emotions were high. Once they were beyond the sight of the drawing-room windows he held out his arm and she slipped her hand into his. The sense of joy and pleasure rioted through her. There was little need for conversation; they seemed to understand each other, breathing in the deep beauty of the night in harmony. From time to time they paused to point out a feature to each other, a black branch or a flower tipped with silver in the street light. The cars swishing past as they neared the central business district formed yet another pattern.

'You've bewitched me, Catriona; I've always enjoyed walking but I've never known it to be such a pleasure.' Cameron spoke as they reached the looming magnificence of the Macarthur building.

'I enjoyed it too. You surprised me; I thought you'd be wanting to summon your chauffeur!'

'My chauffeur?'

'He does go with the job.'

'I had forgotten. He always follows Sir James like a mobile briefcase.' A frown creased his forehead.

'Dad wouldn't like to see him unemployed. The chauffeur probably knows Dad better than most; he's been with us for ten years.'

'I don't want a chauffeur; I prefer to drive.'

'Before you decide give it a trial for two weeks. You may find him definite value, and the two weeks will be long enough for Dad to miss him and the chauffeur to miss Dad! If you approached both men then they'd probably leap at the chance to be back together.'

'Devious diplomacy!'

'Common sense!' she laughed as they walked down to the basement driveway. The large area of garaging contained Rory's sports model and two four-wheel-drive supervisors' utilities. Beyond the pillars was a wall, its surface covered with a bright mural which hid the entry to the long storage area crafted between the apparent wall and the real wall. Cameron opened the door and they walked into the first section, partitioned off for various emergency and site equipment. The second and third bays were filled with files, and it wasn't until they reached the fourth area, a separate room, its door unlocked, that they found the boxed portraits placed carefully on two old oak desks. The first ledgers and the early records were stacked on top of a table.

'These should have been boxed.' Cameron ran a hand along the worn leather binding.

'It's just for two or three days; they're probably safer here than being in the cabinet in the main office. They need a thorough inspection...' dust had coated her fingertips '...and a dusting!'

She opened the stationery file and read one of the printed forms. 'Macarthurs didn't waste print and paper! Listen to this, Cameron!

Dear Sir(s)
    In response to his/their written order of...inst., we have this day shipped by Pass/Goods/Post train these extras to Mr/Messrs advising him/them...'

She chuckled. 'Women didn't exist, according to the grand old company in the...' she checked the paper '...some time between 1920 and 1929.'

'Men then tried to fall into a woman's arms, not her hands,' he laughed. 'A woman's place is in the bedroom and the kitchen!' His hazel eyes were emerald as he looked at Catriona. 'Not a bad idea. I have no trouble picturing you in bed, but I'm not so certain of your abilities in the kitchen...' he dodged as Catriona picked up a ledger '...but, of course, I have respect for your capabilities in business. Any staff member who brings in close on forty-five million dollars' worth of new contracts...'

'You've seen my figures?'

'Not the best one.' He leered lasciviously, breaking into rich mirth at her outraged expression. 'Naturally, I've seen your records. When your father told me he was going to retire I made a point of studying the opposition. You were the one I figured would be my real danger.'

'Me?' She had been surprised when she had been nominated, but to have Cameron call her a danger caught her unawares. She looked at him, a frown creasing itself on her forehead. 'Are you serious?'

'Yes.' His answer was succinct.

'I don't understand, Cameron.'

'Danger? The word comes from the French, originally. It used to be a feudal term and meant the control or power of the right to wood and waters. Appropriate for the daughter of the forestry king.' He leaned against the old desk, his right hand with the thumb tucked under his chin, three fingers folded, the forefinger rubbing his beardline as he studied her. 'But you also fit the modern message...exposure to ruin, destruction, injury, peril, hazard. Aye, Catriona, with your abilities and those blue eyes and that superb, healthy body revealed in that sheath of blue leather, you're definitely my real danger!'

CHAPTER FOUR

'ARROGANT male!' Catriona chuckled. 'And I thought you were serious!'

'I am. After your nomination you held those men in the shadow of your smile. When you smile, Catriona, men feel warmed. It's a special gift.' He was serious, studying her. 'You've a natural talent which has been honed by years of observation and background. Speaking to the directors, you were confident, relaxed. You probably had speech lessons for years.'

She nodded, understanding his point.

'Although you've only been on the board a matter of a few months, those directors know you. Several have been old family friends: apart from me, they have all watched you for years. They are shrewd, wily eagles. They respect you because they've followed your progress. You have a sizeable shareholding which you have increased substantially since you were given control of your trust. Your productivity for the company is only surpassed by Hemi Wilkie, your father and myself. There's a lot of sentiment for the Macarthur name in business. You are very like your father and, from what others say, even more like your grandfather. Apparently he never learnt to tell lies either! People trust you. And you've the tertiary qualifications. It all adds up. Fortunately for me you lack experience, especially in the timber, forestry and brick-making areas. Fortunately for the company you recognised it.'

A faint clang sounded from the street, breaking into their conversation. Dismissing it as traffic noise, Catriona walked towards a battered object, trying to give herself time to assimilate Cameron's words. It was different to hear such an impartial assessment of her place in the company.

'The first concrete-mixer! I can remember Grandad saying he used to turn the handle to earn money in the school holidays. He used to talk about gold-plating it!'

He followed her lead. 'There's a miniature of it on Sir James's desk. It was one of the first things I noticed. A perfect scale model in gold.'

'Dad had it made for Grandfather on his sixtieth birthday.' She drew her jacket closer, aware of the chill. 'It's cold in here.'

'I'll lock up and we'll get going.' Cameron reached for her, putting one arm around her waist. 'But first...' He bent his head, the black hair glinting in the sharp, harsh light of the room, his eyes hidden by the shadows and angles of his face. His kiss touched and retouched her mouth with such gentleness that her heart sang. She pressed closer to him, putting her arms around him, her hands slipping under his jacket feeling his warmth and the firm muscles of his back and shoulders. Revelling in his magic, she opened her mouth to him, kissing him with an abandon which rioted through her. Sensation melted into ecstasy as the kiss continued until she was breathless, desire pounding through her. Shocked by the reality of her own sexuality, she leant against him and instantly he was reassuring, his hands gentle.

'Catriona, you have so much passion and fire,' he murmured, his breath brushing the curls on her shoulder.

'I'm trying to understand.' She shook her head. 'I feel as if I'm losing control.'

The darkness in his eyes was lit in a smile which caressed her. 'Does that trouble you?'

'I'm not sure.' She surprised herself with the statement. Her thoughts were like eager racehorses lined up at an immovable barrier. Wide-eyed, she looked up at him. 'Help me, Cameron.'

'I want you, you want me.' His words were a sigh, but he eased her away so that she was standing alone.

'But it's...impossible...' She put both hands up to smooth back the tumble of black hair.

'Impossible? I would have said just the opposite. Two healthy people; one female, one male.'

'Don't tease me, Cameron. You know what I mean. Yesterday all your name meant was the Black Scot, manager of the Auckland district office. Twenty-four hours ago we'd just met! I'm aware of you as I've never been of anyone else. There's so much attraction. We kiss and I'm...in orbit.'

'The question is whether you remain a floating star or attach yourself to me.'

She began shivering, the trembles shaking her body. 'I can't answer yet.'

'I can show you my AIDS-free certificate. People should protect themselves and their partners.'

She shook her head, realising the distance between them. 'Let's leave it for now.'

He nodded. 'It's too cold in here; undressed, you'd look like a blue baby!' His smile showed in the stripe of light.

Once he had locked the door they passed the storage bays and paused to set the alarm. Hand in hand, they ran through the garage to the driveway, but the sight of the steel grill stopped them.

'No! The security guard has closed the gate.' Catriona looked at her watch. 'It's checked after eleven. I heard the clang of the gate a few minutes ago; I should have realised!'

'And as I haven't worked here I have only the storage key. What about you?'

She laughed. 'At home! We'd better go upstairs and ring them.'

'We'll be unable to get into the main building. Everything will be locked, including the lift and the stairs. But we can make sure.' He led the way to the basement entry. 'One way and another this is quite a day.' Cameron tried the unyielding doors. 'I'll open up the store section again. In the emergency kits there should be the tools I need to rig a bypass for the gate control.' He wrapped his arm around her. 'Not too cold? Take my jacket.'

'I'll keep it in mind!' She pressed the code for the store alarm and the small red light beside it faded. 'We could set off the alarm—it will bring the security firm back.'

'To say nothing of police and possible reporters! I'd rather not.' His Scottish accent was clear in the rolling burr. He walked into the bay and began sorting through a tool-bag. 'Everything here, bar the kitchen sink and a screwdriver!' He bent to the next bag. 'Remind me to get these bags checked regularly. It looks as if someone's nicked a few items from each bag. There are no crescents in this one, or hammers. In an emergency that could cost a life.' He pulled out a set of screwdrivers and selected a small one. 'Just right.' He pocketed a pair of insulated pliers and some wire. Catriona watched as he began to work.

'I'm sure it would have been simpler to hit the alarm!' she laughed as she surveyed the complex wiring.

'It looks worse than it is.'

'Good! I don't want to face an inquisition when we get home late!'

'We won't.'

'Won't be late or won't face an inquisition?' she chuckled as she flicked him with a curl when he bent to the panel.

'This should take me about five more minutes. And the Lady of the Azaleas and Sir James won't care if we spend several hours together. It's their plan, isn't it?'

'Plan? I don't understand.'

'Look, I'll tell you, as I told them, I have no intention of ever marrying again.'

'Fair enough! Your personal life is your business. But what has that got to do with me?'

It was his turn to look up at her, his brow drawn into sharp lines. 'Is it possible you don't know?'

'Don't know what?'

'The marriage plan.'

'What are you talking about?'

'You and me.'

'Us? Marry? I don't even know you!'

'You didn't agree to your parents' scheme? Your shares and my experience. Keeping everything in the family.'

As she took in his meaning she felt stricken, her only object to move away from the hateful suggestion, but the gate was still holding her in. White-faced, she stumbled away, her movements marionette-stiff. She found herself stopped by the far wall of the garage. Hunching up, she allowed the thought to return, forcing herself to replay the speech. Her parents could use her so badly? Put the company before her happiness? Even looking towards Cameron did not help; he stood by the pillar, hard, implacable. He had thought she had agreed... Her cheeks burned when she remembered how she had kissed him with so much abandon. Marry Cameron! To keep the company in the family! There had to be some mistake. She clutched at the idea like a drowning swimmer grabbing at a plank. Trembling with shock and cold, she walked back to Cameron. Her voice when she spoke to him was croaky with strain. 'I want to know exactly what was said. There must be some misunderstanding.'

'When Sir James told me he'd like me for a son-in-law I thought he was joking, his approach was so casual. Your mother was more direct. She said that genetically you and I should combine well to produce healthy, intelligent offspring. She also believes you could have difficulty finding a man who would challenge your potential. She's afraid you might imagine yourself in love with someone unsuitable, such as your much-married Ben Hamilton.'

His words were like blows from a boxer's fists. She leaned against the doorway, her limbs Plasticine-soft. 'As though I were some prime specimen!' she whispered to herself.

'You are! I recall a columnist describing Catriona Macarthur as the young woman with everything: intelligence, health, charm, beauty and, let's not forget, a few millions too.'

'Stop it! Stop it!' Distressed, she could not look at him.

'Whist, lass.' He was in front of her, his hands gentle on her shoulders, wrapping her in his jacket, holding her as the pain spasmed through her. 'I hurt you just now, telling you. I'm sorry; I thought that you were prepared to try to manipulate me for the power and money. That, under that glorious beauty, there was corruption.'

Looking out to the darkness, her eyes were shadowed by the tunnel-like driveway area. 'One of the first things I learnt was that people wanted to make use of me for money or power. When I was a baby a woman with apparently excellent credentials became my nanny. She used to take me into Grandad's office most days. It was only when the grand old company missed out on two major tenders that Grandad realised the nanny was selling company information. I loved Nanny and I was heart-broken when she never came back. At kindergarten I made friends but I also learned about jealousy and spite, and to be wary of some parents.' She tried to smile but it showed her cynicism and bitterness. 'I should be used to it.' After a pause she realised she was gaining comfort from his soothing strokes on her back. She stood up, handing back his jacket, a symbolic action emphasised by her shivers as though she could accept nothing from him. 'I'm sorry; I like you, but you do understand there can be no relationship between us.'

'We can be friends, Catriona.' He slipped the jacket around her, his hands warming her shoulders. 'As for marriage, as far as I am concerned it's not on the agenda. Not now, not ever. Sir James was told that if marriage was a condition then he would have to find someone else to be chairman. And the Lady of the Azaleas was advised to continue hybridising shrubs.' He picked up a screwdriver and moved to the control-panel. 'Let's forget the proposal.'

'How can you make puns about it?'

'To laugh is better than to weep.' He removed several screws. 'If it's any consolation, I believe your parents were aware of the danger you faced, and their concern is understandable. Marriage is a natural step for most people. To find a suitable partner can be difficult, and you have the extra hazard of money in the form of Macarthur shares. There are not many eligible men who could match you financially. You'll have to find someone who's won a lottery or inherited wealth.' He adjusted some wires. 'To make money from scratch takes most millionaires past forty. And most have collected a wife and family by then.'

'That's hateful! There are men to whom my money would make no difference.'

He raised an eyebrow and he continued, smiling. 'You're right! Some monks take a vow of poverty. Pity they take one of chastity, too!'

'You do your own sex an injustice!'

'There haven't been many knights on white chargers rushing around the place lately.' He inserted a screw and tightened it before glancing at her. 'All right, there may be a few immersed or successful in their own field who wouldn't worry if you were dripping diamonds or coals. It would be so much carbon.'

Catriona felt slightly warmed by his observation.

'There are also men to whom the prospect of your money would act like a magnet. I can see from your expression you've run across a few.'

'You speak as if the money and shares were the only interest. I believe in love.'

'Love! You're more naïve than I thought! Romantics just get hurt. Believe me, I know what I'm talking about.'

'You had a bad experience? It can happen. But if I can't marry for love then I won't marry. I'm a career woman and I'm good at my work. At least there I know I can make my own sphere. I've worked harder and longer at the office trying to prove my right to be there and not just because I'm "the Daughter".'

'I wondered what drove you.' Cameron glanced at her. 'Hand me the last screw. Thanks.' He fitted it into position. 'I could be philosophic and point out the screw is useful because it's been shaped for its role...'

She looked at the imprint of the screw on her finger. 'I wonder if the screw screams too.'

'Don't be bitter, Catriona. You'd hurt yourself.' He tugged at the gate and it rolled back. 'Time to go.'

'So much for security!' She watched as Cameron replaced the tools then locked the stores section.

'One of my friends at school was the son of an electronics security manufacturer. I used to work there part-time. It's been useful!'

He shut the gate behind them and reset the control. 'Feels odd to have pliers and wires in my pockets again. Catriona, would you like me to call a taxi?'

'I'd rather walk. I need a little longer.'

The footpath led past the offices and shops and along to the River Avon. 'When I get settled down here I'll build a workshop I can puddle around in. I used to enjoy fixing things.'

'I'll buy you a security firm for Christmas!'

'You're bouncing back again.' His smile was tender. 'A security firm! That's not a silly idea. The company should take a look at the growth and potential in that area, Catriona. It would fit in well with our property and building investments.'

'I'll put a note through to the research team. The Hemingway building will still take my time.'

'Why? The construction is under the architects' control, and the lawyers have signed all the lease agreements; you've done your work, Catriona.'

'There is still a need for liaison, and until it's finished I want to be there for several reasons.'

'Personal and private?'

'Meaning?'

'Ben Hamilton, Catriona? Others have tried to interest Ben in a building contract before and he's always turned it down. Was it some of the Macarthur charm and salesmanship?'

'I dealt direct with the real-estate manager Ben employs. I didn't even meet Ben until one month ago. If you check you'll find he was out of the country. I had been asked to prepare a feasibility study and as part of it I set out options I felt would be of future use to Hemingway Industries. The manager agreed with my assessment, liked the outline and signed the deal.'

'So the office gossips got it all wrong?'

'No.' She answered reluctantly, 'I have been seeing a lot of Ben. We spent hours together working through the building plans with the architect, the landscape artist and the decorator.' She slowed, trying to be analytical. 'Ben and I were on friendly terms rather than business acquaintances from the first moment. We liked each other. He's a little like Rory, so much natural charm that he makes people feel great just by being around. He's fun!'

'And he plays a good game of tennis!'

'When he's serious! You know, I was dreading this weekend, facing the family. I was sure they would have heard about Ben.'

'Well, he did hire the symphony orchestra to serenade you. It was rather a public gesture.'

'Fortunately I was in Palmerston North, so the media couldn't be certain I was the one supposed to be impressed! Ben saw the funny side of it. In a way it was typical of Ben; he's generous, romantic and good-looking, but his attention-span is like a three-year-old's.

He assumed I'd be at my apartment! But he was one man who was impressed with me, not my name and money. Last week one of my friends happened to mention something about Ben's current wife and of course the truth came out. I was shattered.'

'Ben hadn't mentioned his marriages? I wondered.'

'Of course not. I thought I was in love with him.' She was surprised to be able to discuss the situation which had caused her such pain. 'What you said earlier makes sense. I haven't found it easy to have a full relationship with a man. I used to bawl my eyes out on Saturday nights because I didn't have a date. I just wanted an ordinary boyfriend like the other girls had. Someone who cared for me.' She gave a self-deprecating laugh at his sidelong look of disbelief. 'It's true! I used to look in the mirror, wondering what was wrong with me. My looks seem to attract types who want to be seen with the "wealthy, beautiful Miss Macarthur" on their arm. I used to go home furious because all they wanted was a quick conquest they could boast about. They were not interested in what I thought or said. Their values were on a par with a dollar bill and about as reliable.' She shrugged her shoulders. 'Until Ben Hamilton came along. When I found out he was married I thought my heart was broken.'

'And now?'

'Guess I must heal quickly! You arrived and...' she opened her hands in an explanatory gesture '...instant attraction and instant cure!'

'Pleased to be of assistance! But I want you to hand over the Hemingway file.'

Despite his mild tone, Catriona stopped. 'There's no need. Ben and I had a discussion on the subject and he understands.'

'I want you to leave it. Others in the firm can look after it.'

'Are you ordering me?' She broke free of his encircling arm. They had reached the bridge, the lacework of the old iron gleaming cream-white in the street-light. The ripple and rush of water eating at the banks and abutments was noisy in the night quiet.

'It shouldn't be necessary.'

She pulled her jacket fronts together to make up for the loss of warmth. The river, black and silver below them, was no longer the charming, sun-dappled stream. There were currents which could destroy.

Behind them a cinema opened its doors and people gushed out, cars and motorbikes revving into action. Running footsteps came and went as a group of young people, shouting and laughing, headed to a van painted with scenes of mountains and skiing. Their unthinking happiness grated.

Cameron put his arm out to catch at her sleeve, pulling her to a halt. 'Don't fight me, Catriona.'

'You're the chairman!'

'Yes.'

'Great! Just great! You are telling me to leave behind a project which I've spent months organising.' She glared at him. 'We're well into building! I intend to follow it to hand-over day. It's one of our biggest contracts! For me to pass it on to someone else is stupid! Just stupid!'

'Stupid! Are you calling me stupid? You can't even recognise...' He stopped, sobered, as two cats darted, one after the other, along the footpath and disappeared into the bushes surrounding a building. 'Catriona, what are we doing to each other? A pair of alley cats could get together without this fighting.'

She glanced up at him, noting the way the skin around his eyes crinkled into fine lines and, looking at his mouth, she saw the lower lip puckered out of shape in wry amusement.

'Have you heard of the dog in the manger?' she asked. 'If I didn't know better I'd think you were interested in me!'

'Because I have no intention of marrying does not mean I preclude sex.'

'You believe in setting out terms? So do I. Cameron, there's no way there could be a romance between us. You're a cynic; I still hope for love and marriage. We're too different. It just wouldn't work. As though that weren't enough of a barrier, the business would keep on dividing us. As it did a moment ago.' Her head bowed as thoughts tossed in the storms of her mind. Turning, she studied him again. 'At the back of my mind would be a question mark. Would you be interested in me if I didn't have my shares? Have you decided to adapt Mum and Dad's idea? That I could be manipulated to follow your advice?' She saw anger brighten his eyes at the suggestion. 'Now you're furious with me.' She reached out to touch his hand. 'Cameron, I don't mean to insult you. I'm trying to be open and honest. It's hard for me; I've always guarded myself. I've told you things I haven't told anyone else. You disturb me in a way no one has ever done. Yet I scarcely know you. Your work is an open book but there is little written about you as a man. I'm afraid.'

The beeping of the traffic signal telling them to cross set them in motion again.

'Catriona, time should give us trust with each other. There are issues trellised together. We've established that we are attracted to each other.' He looked towards her for confirmation and she gave a reluctant but truthful nod of assent. 'You've just told me that you'd always be wondering if I was interested in you because of your shares... the only answer I can make is that a lot of other people have shares too and I'm not in the least interested in them at a personal level! I'm attracted by you, not your investment portfolio! But I can't pretend you are not Catriona Macarthur—you can only be you! I'm attracted on a physical level, yes, but there's more. We understand the same working environment, the highs and challenges of the business world. You know, too, that I have no time to put into a serious relationship. My new job brings me too many responsibilities.'

'Then that's it, isn't it? I'm not prepared to be some physical panacea. Playing tennis with Rory yesterday, I decided that before I allowed myself to fall in love I was going to analyse the boundaries and stick to the rules.'

'It sounds good... but tell me, did you win that particular game?'

'No!' Catriona chuckled. 'My concentration was not on the game.'

'You didn't lose because Rory was the more powerful and skilled player?' Cameron's eyes, black in the streetlight shadows, studied her.

'Point taken. You can be sure that when I find the man who is right for me I'll be giving the matter my close attention.'

'He won't stand a chance!' His teeth were white. 'Let's say goodbye to what might have been. Come here, you gorgeous, kissable creature!' Without giving her time to think, his arm wrapped her closer and his head bent to kiss her quick protest into silence. Automatically she found her hands moving around him, winding herself closer to him, enjoying the sensuous pleasure which entangled them. She felt the touch of his lips on her cheek and her hair and drew a sharp breath when he began nuzzling her ear, his hands on her skin tracing whirlpools of desire until she was conscious only of him.

The bright flash of a camera broke the moment.

'Look this way, thank you, Miss Macarthur.' Again the light dazzled, and Catriona put up her hands to shield her eyes.

Cameron put her away from him. 'Stop it! Who the——?'

'It's Mr McDougall, isn't it?' The reporter and photographer belatedly introduced themselves. 'We were doing a piece on the safety aspect of walking the streets at night, but then we recognised Miss Macarthur... You're taking over the company as chairman; could it be better described as a merger, perhaps?'

'My chairmanship has nothing to do with any relationship between Miss Macarthur and myself. Our private lives are of no concern to anyone else.' Cameron was apparently controlled, but the anger was evident to Catriona in the rolled burr in his voice. 'I'll thank you to leave us alone.'

'Miss Macarthur, how would you describe your friendship with the new chairman of the grand old company?'

Catriona looked around for a taxi but a familiar limousine cruising towards them gave her confidence. 'The time-honoured phrase, gentlemen: we are just good friends.'

Sir James's chauffeur opened the doors, enabling them to escape. 'I suppose it would be useless offering to buy the negatives,' Cameron growled as the car carried them towards the house.

'Money can buy a lot, but not that pair. They are more interested in their work than the social round. If you'd offered them a bribe that fact and the enlarged pic of us kissing would have been plastered over the front page. With luck they'll stumble on another story and decide we're not newsworthy.'

'I don't know when I've been so furious and so helpless.' He smashed one fist into the other in a gesture of impotent frustration. 'I'm sorry, Catriona.'

'Given what you told me earlier, my father isn't likely to insist on pistols at dawn!'

'It wasn't your parents I was concerned about.'

'Me?' She opened her hands wide as if she could not care. 'It was a kiss. Hail and farewell!'

She kept her expression calm, unwilling for him to see how much the kiss had meant to her. Given their conversation, what could she say? That she had fallen in love with him? She knew his conditons and she knew her own morality. Why couldn't she have fallen in love with a man who was free and ready to form a lasting relationship, to have children, to establish a home? Was that so very much to ask? Why did life have to be so complicated?

'Yes, you're right, Catriona.' Stiff, he moved towards the window, isolating himself in the spacious interior of the limousine. Catriona felt betrayed by the new distance between them. Heartsore, she felt it was a gap which would never be bridged.

CHAPTER FIVE

JUST GOOD FRIENDS? The cliché bannered the large photo. The newspaper's picture was graphic, showing Cameron looking into Catriona's eyes, their faces barely apart, an intimate moment captured by the camera. Dismayed, she read the article beside the picture; of Cameron's and her own achievements little had been stated, and the reporter's succinctness was cleverly damaging, the implication being that Sir James Macarthur's unexpected retirement and Cameron's vote to chairman of one of the nation's companies might be explained by the picture. Catriona's blue eyes shadowed as she skimmed the paragraph again.

Crushing the paper down, she looked towards the guest suite across the lawns, the curtains lazily floating forwards and backwards on the slight easterly. 'Is Cameron awake?' she asked the housekeeper setting the breakfast trays.

'Awake! He went off to the gym at six o'clock as he always does. Before the paper arrived!' The housekeeper added, smiling, 'I'm very glad for you, Catriona. Just what your parents were hoping for, a match between you.'

Catriona felt helpless. 'But we hadn't even met till the night before last!'

'How much time do you need to fall in love?' The housekeeper began slicing grapefruit. 'I like Cameron. I think he'll take care of you. He's growing into a forest

73

giant, but he's carrying a load of supplejack. Just don't get entangled without protecting yourself.'

'Not a chance! I'm a career girl, remember!'

The housekeeper put down the teapot. 'Don't I know it! You should be having fun! Now, don't you look at me like that! It's time you thought about finding a good man and marrying him. You might look young, but I've been with this family twenty years and you had your third birthday when I arrived. You're almost twenty-four!'

'You too!' Catriona groaned. 'There's more to life than marriage!'

'There's more to life than studying and making money, too. Now sit down and eat some breakfast.'

Catriona shook her head, her decision made. 'No; I was going to stay for the weekend, but with this... I'll go back to Wellington before Cameron returns. Would you tell my parents?'

'Running away? You'd be making a mistake, Catriona.'

'I've already made it.' Catriona tore the photo from the newspaper and pocketed it. She gave the house-keeper a hug. 'There's a Press conference on Monday and the quickest way to end the rumour is for me to leave. The suggestion that Cameron got the job because of me is outrageous.' She glanced at the clock on the kitchen wall. 'There's a flight in an hour's time. I wonder if Rory could take me to the airport.'

'Rory! He's likely to be asleep until midday! But I saw the chauffeur a few moments ago. He'll take you.'

When Catriona reached her apartment in Wellington she was defeated, her emotions depressed. She looked around the flat, aware for the first time that its designer interior grated, its sterile artistry showing off the revival

Bauhaus style, a subtle mockery of her own emptiness. For relief she turned to the large windows showing the familiar harbour scene: the sea, ships, and the quays. Roads veined from the wharves, led to warehouses and the retail heart and the high-rise office blocks, then arteried back to the waterfront. The vidid blue sea, sparkling with the brightness of the reflected sun in ten million wavelets, lay contentedly somnolent, contained by the scrub- and bush-covered hills. Houses flowered, sprawling over the ground, others clinging to the curve of the hill, a few standing sturdily in self-righteous straight lines.

Below her a young couple were walking on the sandy beach of the bay, and when they stopped to kiss under the fronds of a tree, believing themselves hidden, she felt a physical ache for Cameron. Doubt sat on her shoulder, echoing the housekeeper's words: 'How much time do you need to fall in love?'

Wandering round the apartment, trying to ignore thoughts of Cameron proved impossible. By closing her eyes she could feel his arms close about her and his mouth brush her own ... She stood up and in doing so knocked over her suitcase, laddering her tights. Grimacing, she seized the case and unpacked it, the action keeping the teasing thoughts checked. Once the room was tidy and the case away she found herself trying to guess what Cameron was doing. What would he have made of her sudden flight? Should she have discussed it with him? Her parents! What would Cameron say to them?

Debating silently, she went to the telephone to call him but replaced the receiver before she touched the memory button. By leaving she had shown him she wasn't

interested in a short-term affair, and hadn't Cameron
ruled out a long relationship?

Unable to stand her circle of thought, she changed
and pulled on shorts, top and running shoes. A jog
around the next few bays and back would push away
the thoughts of Cameron as she would have to concentrate on the exercise. Within a few minutes she was side-
stepping down the narrow path to the ocean, and once
on the sand her body began to pound out a blocking
rhythm. At the end of the bay she avoided the rocks,
crossing to the footpath, her feet padding a drum-beat,
slowing or speeding as she gained clear space. She began
to feel better, the exercise freeing her of the earlier ten-
sions. After more than an hour she slowed to a walk;
hot, sticky, her hair curling damply, she realised she had
covered far more territory than usual. Her path had led
her direct to the exposed southern shore where the gales
of Cook Strait powered the sea into constant battle
against the land, the crashing of the waves on to the
rocks forming a background rhythm to the wind's el-
dritch song.

Conscious of the power of nature around her, the
balance of sea, land and wind, she stood gazing towards
the South Island, although the hills of the Sounds were
not visible. She could see the clear parallel with her own
feelings. They were there whether she acknowledged them
or not. Cameron had altered her life, her priorities. She
refused to believe she was in love with him, but she would
admit his touch effloresced her being. What she would
do about the situation remained a puzzle. She retraced
her steps, and her energy was diminished by the time
she reached the bay below her home. An empty seat
under the shade of a tree tempted her. Stretching, calf
muscles already protesting, she sat down, mechanically

pushing aside a local newspaper someone had dropped. Her hands froze as she recognised the photo of Cameron and herself, headlined, ROMANTIC MERGER FOR GRAND OLD COMPANY? The realisation that the photo had been picked up by the capital's Press meant she would face considerable teasing from her friends. To tell them she had just met Cameron would only make the jocularity and speculation worse!

The telephone was ringing when she reached the flat. She ignored it, knowing it would flick over to the answer system, and she was unprepared to speak to friends or reporters asking about her relationship with Cameron. What could she say?

If she told them that Cameron was one of the few men, apart from Rory and her father, with whom she was able to discuss her feelings with complete honesty it would not help the situation. If she explained that the kiss had been meant as a farewell for what might have been then the photograph itself would convict her. Everyone would ask why. What could she say? That her parents had precluded any romance by their wish to see them married? That Cameron had decided he would never marry again? Why? And what had happened when he'd touched her? Did she dare to remember the blaze of intense emotion which had flared like sky rockets when they'd kissed? Fireworks lasted only a few seconds too! By flying north she had confirmed their decision to finish the romance before it had gone too far. She sighed, correcting herself; from the first kiss it was too late. From the buffet she picked up the newspaper photo she had ripped out. With one finger she traced the outline of his head as though by doing so she could turn him around to read his expression. Had she fled because she was afraid of his attraction or her own?

Again the imperious shrilling of the telephone sounded and her shoulders relaxed when her answer-phone switched on, only to tense as she heard Cameron's voice. Fingers tentative, she picked up the phone. 'I'm here, Cameron.'

'Catriona? Are you all right?'

Joy danced in her blue eyes at hearing the warmth and anxiety in his deep voice. 'Yes, I'm fine.' She heard her own routine response, 'No, that's scarcely accurate,' and struggled to explain. 'I feel like milk being whizzed in a shake machine, mixed up and uncertain. Events have been happening too fast for me. I intended to make it easier for you with the Press conference, but part of me admits I ran away. Incidentally, the Wellington papers have picked up the photo too.'

'It will be forgotten in a couple of days. I'm sorry you left so soon.'

'The implication that I was the reason for your promotion was unfair, Cameron.'

'I'm a big laddie; sandflies of speculation only irritate. It was you I was concerned about. I did ring earlier.'

'I went out for a run; it lasted longer than I'd intended.'

'The trouble with running away from a problem is that sooner or later you have to turn and face it. And sometimes the last steps back are harder because of the distance you covered in the first place.'

'Philosophy is not exactly what I need right now.'

'A masseur, perhaps? Tight leg muscles?'

She could hear the warm chuckle in his voice.

'If I were with you I could massage your legs, but,' his tone sobered, 'I think that it's just as well we're apart. You're a beautiful, intelligent woman, and so sexy...you're the embodiment of every adolescent fantasy I ever had... but you want and need more than a casual affair. Yet I can't afford to think of putting time into a serious relationship. I've made that mistake before... Until we get the new infrastructure in place I'll be working long hours. We made the right decision last night. That was to forget our attraction.'

'Forget?' Her voice cracked on the word as though it echoed the break opening in her emotions. 'What was there to forget?'

'You understand.'

Her blue eyes were filling with tears but she forced her mouth into a smile. 'Of course. Just too much hassle. This way we can limit our communication to work.' She could feel the brittleness and knew she could keep up the charade no longer. 'Bye, Cameron.' The tears were dripping down her cheek and falling on to her hand as she replaced the receiver. She looked at the clear diamonds of pain, then brushed her fingers against her eyes, sniffing in an ineffectual attempt to stop the flow.

'Miss Macarthur, the chairman on line two.'

Catriona acknowledged the message and reached for the telephone, her mind swinging from the figures in front of her to Cameron. It had been more than two weeks since she had left Christchurch, and after the first speculative media reports of a romance the knowledge that she had returned to Wellington had allowed the story to dry up for lack of evidence. Fed by the public-relations department, Cameron's first media meeting had been successful, his career and plans featuring prominently in the business pages. She had read them, eyes avidly searching for gleanings which would add to her own knowledge of the man, but they did not help. She scanned the photos of him but they were all the same,

an official release in which Cameron was dressed in a
dark suit, his black hair suitably ordered into sub-
mission, his eyes calm, reflective, and his bearing having
the quiet authority he wore as easily as his suit. Of
passion or disordered emotion there was no sign.

'Miss Macarthur, the chairman on line two!'

The secretary's urgent repetition penetrated her
thoughts and she grappled with her feelings in an effort
to regain control. 'Good morning, Cameron; Catriona
speaking.'

'The weekly reports show you are working on the
Hemingway building. Is there a reason?'

'A reason?' Catriona repeated his words, her disappointment catching at her as she berated herself for the
quick hope. He hadn't even wished her a good morning!

'We're ahead of schedule by nearly five days.'

'As I said, I read the report. There appears no need
to have you redoing others' work. At the end of the
month I want you to report to the board on milling the
Oranga block we gained when we took over Lumber
South.'

'Cameron, are you serious? You know what the
Hemingway building means to me. I know every sup-
plier and subbie on the job. The reason it's ahead of
schedule is because I'm using——'

'Hand it over. I need your input on the Lumber South
block.'

'Milling? I've never pretended to be expert——'

'You should be. At last month's directors' meeting
you didn't vote on the question. Checking back on earlier
meetings, I found you abstained from the vote on milling
or followed your father's lead. As a director you have
a duty to inform yourself.'

Her project was sliding from her control and she made an effort to grab it. 'As soon as the Hemingway building is finished I'll set aside time to make a thorough——'

'Catriona, you're off the Hemingway project. I want a complete report regarding the consequences and the potential profits or loss of milling the Oranga Lumber South block at the next directors' meeting. You've already got copies of the file. Use whatever facilities you must—you haven't much time. Good morning.'

The click of the receiver stung her like a wasp. Mutinously she glared at the telephone. 'And I thought I might have been in love with you!' She saved and copied her computer file and took out the floppy disks, putting one in her drawer and then giving the other, with explicit instructions, to a member of their construction office. Still resentful, she called her secretary to bring her the Oranga Lumber South file. The unopened pages were a silent reprimand but the aerial photos of the place intrigued, showing a small lake fed from glacial snow in the mountains and the ground covered with primeval bush. It looked so beautiful that she felt remorse that she was studying it with a view to learning the possible profit milling would bring Macarthur's. Did it have to be milled? Was that the wisest choice for the remote heart of the land? She flicked the bulky file of reports and began to read. An hour later she pushed back her chair, realising she was out of her depth—she needed a tutor. Her father, Cameron and Hemi Wilkie were the acknowledged experts on milling. She could not face daily contact with Cameron—her emotions were too fragile— and if she went to her father she could not hope to avoid meeting Cameron. Family phone calls had told her he was no longer staying in the guest suite but he called to

the house frequently to consult with Sir James. Her hand
went to the telephone and she rang Hemi.

At three-thirty she headed north to meet him. By seven
she was settling into the company's Palmerston North
staff apartment, Hemi having already left her with an
outline of facts and figures which threatened to engulf
her. After a week of fourteen-hour days of intensive
study broken by early-morning or evening runs or a game
of tennis she was able to follow why her father and Hemi
had made past decisions on milling.

'That's good, Catriona.' Hemi finished reading the
précis of facts on the Oranga block he had asked her to
prepare. 'Tomorrow we see the reality; we'll fly south
to inspect the Oranga block. On the way we'll check our
pinus radiata Nelson forest; you haven't been there for
four months and the new equipment has not increased
the productivity as much as the manager estimated. After
lunch we'll head to Hokitika and look at the bush-milling
plant operation. You were still a teenager the last time
you saw one. Then on to Oranga. Any objection to
spending two or three days on site?' Hemi's brown eyes
gleamed. 'The trout-fishing sounded lip-smacking!'

Catriona smiled 'It's fine with me! Just promise you'll
clear my cabin of rats and wetas. And we share the
cooking!'

'It may not be too bad; there is a guide-cum-caretaker.'

'You've already packed your fishing gear?'

'Best excuse I've had in years. A spot which should
be crowded with trout! The only way in or out is a four-
day tramp through bush, or else by helicopter.'

'I used to love the bush...' She picked up the thick
file on her desk. 'The staff have already compiled conflicting reports, some regarding the proposed clearing as
unjustifiable, others stating the opposite.' She shrugged

her shoulders. 'The ecological report worries me. There are several potential trouble-spots near the lake. The Soil Conservation and Rivers Control Act has to be remembered. Then there are the native birds; some are on the threatened list.'

'Not forgetting the existence of several species of rare plants! And the boundary shared on two sides with a national park!' Hemi passed her another paper listing instructions. 'Here's the plan. A staff car will pick you up at six in the morning and drop you at the airport. I'll meet you, we'll take a scheduled service to Nelson, then it'll be company plane and helicopter.'

'I'll be ready. Will your wife come with us? She's such fun.'

'She's too much a fan of civilisation—in particular, flush loos!' Hemi glanced at his watch. 'I'd better get home, but before I go you could be interested in a fax I received from Wellington.'

Catriona grinned as she pounced on the report on the Hemingway building. 'You're an angel!' Waving goodbye to Hemi, she began reading the daily computer print-outs. The reports showed everything was flowing on as planned. It left her feeling ambivalent; naturally she was pleased that the team and programme she had set up was working well, but it was annoying to have proved Cameron had been right: she wasn't needed on the project!

'In the Nelson block you saw sustainable reserves; we cut, we replant, a natural cycle.'

Hemi spoke crisply against the noise of the helicopter. Catriona nodded, sparing a glance for the bush they were flying over, then returned her attention. If she had to make the report for Cameron she had to concentrate.

'The Hokitika block was native bush; it had been partially milled a hundred years ago but there was enough beech to chip to make it a profitable addition to the balance sheets. We'll grass it for pasture and re-sell. The Oranga block is old growth, many trees being more than a thousand years old...' Hemi looked up as the pilot began turning the helicopter back towards the direction from which they had come.

'There's a radio message from head office.' The pilot looked sympathetic. 'I'm sorry, Mr Wilkie; your wife's been taken to hospital with an asthma attack. I've instructions to get you back on the double to Haast; the company plane will fly you direct to Palmerston North.'

'Hemi, I'm sorry.' Catriona placed her right hand along Hemi's as the healthy colour ebbed from his face, leaving him a yellow-grey. 'By now she will be receiving the best possible care. When you reach her she'll be sitting up, ready to reassure you.'

The brown eyes misted. 'My wife is like the rata bloom in the forest. She's so bright and beautiful...'

'And one of the bravest people I know,' Catriona encouraged. 'She has a lot worth fighting for... a husband whom she is still in love with and who loves her after more than twenty years of marriage! I envy you.' She spoke softly but it was the truth. Even a few days with Hemi and his wife had shown her how empty her own life seemed. It had also established that Cameron was not the man for her; she wanted a man who would, like Hemi, put his personal relationships first, ahead of the demands of his work.

She could hear the pilot talking to the control tower and knew that soon they would be landing. She took the papers from Hemi's hands and stowed them in her briefcase.

'Miss Macarthur, head office wants you to wait here until Mr McDougall arrives.' The pilot listened to the radio again. 'He'll meet you here in an hour.'

'Cameron's coming?' She heard her voice crack.

'You could be in for an interesting time!' Hemi, recovered from his shock, managed a grin. 'The Black Scot is quite a bushman! I'm sorry I won't be there to chaperon.'

'Don't worry, he's too like my father, work being everything.'

'Should I say something about stones and glasshouses?'

'That's not fair! I care about people. Cameron's a systems man.'

'Does he trust them because they can't let him down or because he can't let them down?'

While she was considering Hemi's comment the pilot set the helicopter on to the tarmac like a giant dragonfly alighting on a lily pad. The roar of the dying rotors swung in on them as the door was opened, and for a few moments all was bustle as Catriona helped Hemi transfer to the familiar plane. As it rose she followed her pilot's suggestion to wait on a bench while he refuelled. With mixed feelings she pulled out her notes; Cameron would not find her short on facts and projected estimates. She had to overcome the tendency to think about him, but by the time his plane touched down she had briefed herself again on the projected results and checked and rechecked her make-up and hair. Walking to the helicopter, she noted that the pilot had the rotors spinning and the door open, and as she climbed aboard her hair was whipped into a frenzy of curls by the down draught. Regretting the necessity, she tied it into place with a twisted scarf, her fingers mechanical, while scanning the tarmac for Cameron. When they met she would be courteous, businesslike, secure in her own dignity. She visualised graciously extending her hand, cool and impervious to his attraction.

Her fantasy vanished when he appeared—the contrast with the business-suited man she knew and the red-bush-shirted, shorts-clad and boot-wearing rugged male who appeared was total. He looked like a deerstalker or a fisherman rather than a company chairman, but his charm was in evidence as he laughed with two of the staff, and his farewell wave to them as he angled towards the waiting craft sent a pang of foreboding in her emotions. She watched as he slung a backpack on to the floor, carefully stowed a long thin box, then hefted himself on board, and acknowledged the pilot, greeting him by name and a swift, 'Take her up!' Buckling himself into the seat beside her, he smiled, and the sudden sensation of the earth moving as the chopper rose found Catriona breathless, all her calm lost.

'Good afternoon, Catriona. Sorry to hold you up—this trip was advanced by four days when I was rung by Hemi's lad. The latest news on Hemi's wife is that her condition has stabilised.'

'That's good.' Catriona found her answer stilted.

'Bit of a rush leaving; fortunately I'd prepared my fishing gear the other night.'

The laughter in his eyes left her bereft of speech, her heartbeat racing, her fingers white-knuckled as she gripped the safety-belt, relieved that the clipboard on her lap hid her tension. The knowledge that he had planned to visit the spot after she had left scratched her feelings. 'There was no need for you to change your plans on my account. I have the facts and figures I need.'

'We haven't an inexhaustible supply of choppers, and you can't learn to check the bush figures on your own. I couldn't guarantee Hemi's return.'

Not trusting her tight, thick throat with speech, she nodded, wondering how she could have been so asinine as to think that Cameron had taken advantage of the change in plans to give himself time with her. Tears prickled in her blue eyes and she turned away, almost pressing her nose against the window, desperate to ensure her feelings were held in check. How did Cameron have the power to hurt so easily? Why was she so vulnerable where he was concerned? Outwardly stoic, she gazed at the scenery, mile after mile of beech-covered hills and snow-topped mountains, held back from the sea by the thin line of sand.

'Today we had marvellous views as we crossed the Alps,' Cameron's voice was impersonal. 'Crest after crest of jagged snow-covered peaks, like waves of the sea.'

Recovering from the buffeting of the emotional winds, she strived for a similar tone. 'One of the Maori names was Tirotiromoana.' She said the word with full resonance, savouring it, then, seeing his expression, she translated, '"To see the sea again." On a fine winter's day from the plains the mountains do look like giant waves breaking white.'

'I'd remembered your beauty but forgotten how sensuous your voice sounded.' Keen, intelligent hazel eyes studied her. 'I wish I weren't so attracted to you, Catriona.'

She frowned; he wasn't keeping to the business plan she had set herself. 'I'm sure you'll be able to ignore my presence—you have for the past three weeks.'

'I have?' A smile was lurking in his eyes. 'Why do you think I was taking such an interest in what a particular member of the board was doing?'

'You didn't let it stop you from ordering me around.'

'You weren't needed on the Hemingway building. Human resources are valuable.' His smile softened the terse explanation. 'Besides, from the conflicting reports, I believe the Oranga block deserves the best brains available.'

'Is that supposed to appease me?'

'It's my explanation.'

The light in his hazel eyes danced like sunshine on a wind-rustled forest pool, and she drew a quick breath as her emotions roller-coasted. 'Don't make the situation difficult for me, Cameron. I was looking forward to seeing this part of the country.'

'You're the one who might make problems for me; your physical attraction is more than appealing—it's sensational!'

'I thought you'd already decided that a relationship isn't advisable.'

'But you smell as enticing as a delicately perfumed flower, your skin has the soft glow of a petal and——'

'You're but a poor moth, doomed to flutter at the window!' Bravery encouraged her chuckle.

'I deserved that,' he laughed. 'Speaking of windows, look out at the view! Where's my camera?' He leaned forward and spoke to the pilot, and they slowed to a hover, allowing Cameron, having retrieved his camera, to work his way back beside her.

'I'll move—the best views are from this side,' she offered.

'Stay there; it gives me an excuse to get close to you.'
He smiled, suiting action to the word, half kneeling to
line up a shot. 'Just so beautiful.'

His voice was a soft breath in her ear, and she did not
dare move in case they touched. Too aware of Cameron,
she could hardly take in the river edging eternally from
mountain to sea. Her sophistication crumbling, she
reinforced it with over-bright information. 'The Haast
highway was opened to allow easy access to the magnificence of...' her voice was dropping '...the south-
west coast...' She gave up the lecture when his body
steadied against hers, and she could feel the movements
in his arms as his hands adjusted the camera.

'That's better!' He clicked off another series of shots.

She could feel the slight scratchiness of his shaven
beardline, smell the subtle aftershave warmed by the heat
of his body, and the sensations were rushing through
her, setting up powerful messages. As he leant his body
even closer, slipping his left arm right around her to
reposition the camera, she stiffened.

'You don't mind, do you?' He was apparently un-
moved by their proximity.

'No, no, of course not.'

'Little liar!' he murmured as she turned, holding her
imprisoned with his left arm while his left hand stroked
the curve running from behind the lobe of her right ear
to the protection of her V-fronted shirt. The gesture was
so erotic that it took seconds to notice she was staring
at the back of an empty camera, a charade prop to allow
him to hold her!

'You've taken more liberty than film!' She pushed him
back towards his seat and signalled the pilot to continue
the flight. Her own emotions were whirling up one

minute and down the next. Which was nonsensical, of course. Hadn't they already agreed there was no chance in any relationship other than work? So what difference would two days in the bush make?

CHAPTER SIX

'WE'RE heading inland,' Cameron commented as he checked a map. 'Shouldn't be too long now, and then I'll fish you up a trout for your dinner!'

'Sounds good!' Her confidence regained, Catriona found it easy to talk to Cameron, pointing out landmarks as the terrain changed. A river led them into a primeval land, a world of green striped with silver waterfalls, scarred with black patches where the thin soil and its covering of bush had been ripped from the granite or gneiss by the rain. Away from the coast the land opened again in bush-covered flats, then revealed more steep ranges up to the mountains.

'We are at the edge of the block now,' the pilot informed them. 'The north boundary follows the course of the river then the line of the lake and over the next two valleys. Do you want to fly over it all now?'

Cameron glanced at Catriona and spoke for both of them. 'No, just take us to the camp. Tomorrow we can make a better inspection.'

Within minutes they had landed, and Catriona looked around as she stepped out. The forest-edged small lake, its backdrop of snow-covered mountains, the foothills covered with beech and foregrounded by a wide plateau of rimu and totara, was the terrain the photos had led her to expect, but the reality was so vivid, so much more spectacular. 'It's beautiful! It really is Oranga!' Seeing Cameron's head turn in question, she hesitated before attempting to translate, 'A place of healing, of well-being, a place to take time out. It's a concept, really.'

Cameron nudged her into awareness of a man approaching. 'I can't say welcome.' The middle-aged man regarded them with a speaking sniff of disapprobation. 'You must be Miss Macarthur and Mr McDougall; I'm the guide, cook, caretaker, whoever. Make yourself at home—after all, according to the bit of paper, it is yours.' He waved in the general indication of the bush and went on to greet the pilot, his change of manner verging on the comical.

'Hardly enthusiastic, but, given the circumstances, predictable.' Cameron looked where the guide had grudgingly indicated. 'I expect the cabin will be a rough diamond too.'

'A jewel, certainly!' Catriona, having moved closer to the bush, saw past the forest giants into a small clearing. An architect-designed lodge, built of stained, rough-sawn timber with large windows to catch sun and view, sat camouflaged under its roof of olive-green. To one side a large glasshouse revealed dim outlines of tomatoes, and rows of vegetables.

'I don't believe it!' Cameron ejaculated. 'The guy who prepared the briefing sheet for the camp needs investigation, describing it as a down-at-heel bush cabin! What are you laughing about?'

'Don't you see? It was the caretaker-cum-guide who wrote that particular page. We presumed it was "down at heel", a typing error, but in fact the report said "down at hill". And he's right. Look at the level of the land; there is a slight angle downhill to the lake, and see the sign above the door...'

'Bush Cabin!' As he read it Cameron's eyes lit with laughter. 'A dream home in the middle of the wilderness! The original sales brief documented a fishing lodge built for the owner of Lumber South. I expected something substantial but after reading the separate brief... It must have been a blow to the guide when we took over Lumber South. It's obvious he loves the place.'

'He's probably alarmed that we intend to mill.'

'Looking at those stands of rimu and totara, I can see he has reason. The report on them was accurate. They're a prospective gold-mine.'

'They're so magnficent, though. Just look at them, Cameron!'

'Does beauty have a price? Can you put it on a balance sheet?'

The savagery of the guide's words and appearance startled them.

'It has value beyond rubies.' Cameron spoke with a gentleness which impressed Catriona. 'I realise this is difficult for you. Without coming here we would not have been able to assess all aspects. It is our duty to the shareholders to invest their money and plant in a responsible and profitable manner, as it is our duty to the staff to provide work.'

'And if that means destroying one of nature's undefiled spots you'll go ahead. See those totara over on the other side... they've been estimated at more than twelve hundred years of age. There's only a handful but they can be chipped and sent off to——'

'We don't chip totara—it's too valuable. Tell me about the fishing.' Cameron looked towards the lake. 'Would it be possible to catch a trout for our dinner, do you think?'

Catriona saw the dilemma on the man's face. He wanted to carry on his lecture, but Cameron's quiet manner and the question on fishing warred with a desire to boast about the lake's angling potential.

'What sort of a rod have you there, Mr McDougall?'

Cameron opened the long, thin box and the glow in the man's eyes as he handled the pieces, delicately fitting them together and testing the balance, was a seal of approval. He sniffed, more as a habit, Catriona realised, than as condemnation. 'You'd better have a cup of tea, then I'll take you out.'

Inside the house, Catriona smiled with pleasure at the visual harmony of the décor with the glimpses of the lake showing through the windows of the main lounge, a simple, massive room with a billiard table to one side, a large open fireplace of stone, and a luxurious, inviting deep-padded suite of reclining rocker chairs and a bed-sized settee. Two black Labrador dogs lay on the sheepskin mat in front of the fireplace, their faces full of yearning curiosity.

'What wonderful dogs! So well trained!' Catriona turned to the owner. 'Do you mind if I pay them some attention?' She could hardly have picked on a better subject.

'They're two of the best, I reckon. Told them to stay in case you didn't like dogs wandering around. Some people don't.' He turned to the two sets of golden eyes. 'It's OK, fellas.'

Released, the dogs bounded towards them, eagerly accepting Catriona's and Cameron's pats and praise, and including the pilot in their finger-sniffing welcome.

'I'll show you the rooms.' The caretaker opened first one door and then gestured Cameron to the adjoining one and the pilot to one on the opposite side. 'Cuppa on the table in five minutes.'

Catriona smiled as she walked into her bedroom, the knotted-pine walls and the *en suite* bathroom with its luxurious shower and toilet being the opposite to remembered bush camps with their hosepipe showers and long drop or chemical toilets. She hung up her clothes in the dressing area, noting the smooth glide of the joinery as she unpacked her toiletries and make-up. A check on her watch told her the time was up, and she returned to the main room in time to see the caretaker being pouring the tea. Cameron was there, and when he met her gaze his smile was like the warmth of the sun breaking through clouds on a wet day.

'Coming fishing, Catriona?'

'No, thanks, I've done enough sitting in a cramped space for one day. Besides, you might ask me to row the boat! I think I'll go for a wander.'

A sniff of disapproval made her glance at the caretaker.

'I'll be sensible; I'll stay within sight of the lake.'

'Catriona, if you go three feet into the bush you won't be able to see the lake.' Cameron spoke crisply. 'I'd appreciate it if you stay at the camp; otherwise I'll put off the fishing so you can have the guide.'

'That's emotional blackmail.'

'Call it what you like—you're not going to wander around alone; outside that door is primeval forest.'

'I'm not a baby! I grew up having holidays in the bush.' Her indignation petered out. She knew as well as Cameron her father's dictum, 'Never alone unless radio-equipped and on familiar terrain.' Gritting her teeth, she tried to hide her chagrin.

Cameron smiled. 'We'll be back in half an hour—that's a promise!'

'Only because it will be dark by then!' She found his boyish enthusiasm contagious as the pilot and caretaker joined in discussing lures, flies and techniques. The tea was finished quickly, and she accompanied them down to the lake and around a corner of the track.

'The rowboat,' Cameron laughed as a sleek jet boat swayed slightly, tethered to a concrete and post jetty. 'How many other surprises do you think your wilderness offers?'

'One or two,' the caretaker admitted as he held the boat steady.

Cameron turned to her. 'The monster sandflies will get you if you stay here, love. Come on, Catriona, there's plenty of room.'

He had called her 'love'. Of course, it had slipped out and he had corrected himself almost in the same breath, but he had said the word... Almost floating, she stepped down to the boat.

Joy rushed through her like the wind, flicking her curls into a thousand tendrils as they sped across the lake. Its mirror surface was chopped into silver fragments, only to re-piece itself as the guide cut the motor. He motioned for silence and they drifted gradually into a small bay created by a creek. Catriona lay back against the padded comfort as she took in the soft evening beauty of the lake losing itself in the depths of the mountains. The air tasted like a crisp wine, fresh and with a tang of sharp chill. Listening, Catriona realised she could hear none of the sounds of machines, just the orchestra of nature's evening overture, the first calls of the night birds and their faint scratchings on the forest floor. A plop as a fish jumped beside them set the men into a flurry of activity. She shuddered at the thought of the noise the

mill would cause. The chainsaws' whines would scream
the forest's violation.

'Ever tried fishin', Miss?' The guide rested a rod in
her hands.

'Years ago! Never with any success, though.' She
flicked the line on to the water in obedience to his direc-
tions but her vision returned to the romantically coloured
pink, mauves and purple of the twilight sky and bush-
covered hills. It reminded her of the paintings of an
earlier period, colourings she had scorned as being too
beautiful to be real. What would it look like when the
bush had gone? A barren wasteland? Hillsides eroded
to grey rock or clay? The reports had said the land would
not suit grassland pasture. Replanting into pinus radiata
like the Nelson forest? But would it regrow economi-
cally? She tried painting the hills in rows of bright emerald but the thousand tones of the bush defeated her.
She was surprised when she felt a pull on the line and
she stared, disbelieving, as the reel began spinning, the
nylon thread racing away.

'You've got one, Catriona?' Cameron hastily wound
in his line and the pilot followed suit. 'Now start quietly
to wind up a little, bring the pressure on, then ease it.
He'll start to run and you don't want to lose him...'

Twenty minutes later, her back, leg and arm muscles
tight with the unaccustomed strain, Catriona was still
following the plentiful advice, easing and rewinding the
fish, but she could feel the end of the battle. With de-
cison made she looked at Cameron.

'I want to release it. We can eat bread and butter for
dinner!'

Ahead of her the water bubbled as a giant trout arced
up, flashing gleaming brown as it jumped, then changed

direction. Catriona felt her line quiver and the fish was gone.

'You've lost him, tiger! He was a beauty!'

'Who was playing with whom? A grand fight, though.' The guide was checking through his box of lures. 'We won't see him for a day or two, I'm picking. But as it happens I caught a couple of trout just before you arrived. It's too dark to carry on. I'll take you fishing at dawn, if you want to go...'

'You're on!' Cameron and the pilot spoke simultaneously but Catriona shook her arms and rubbed her wrists. 'Think I'll stay in bed. I never realised fishing was such hard work!'

The roar of the boat's jets sent them speeding back towards the lights on the lodge, and within a few minutes the precious gear was hooked in place and they went to wash for dinner. Catriona showered quickly in an attempt to ease her aching muscles, but the effort of drying her hair was too much.

'I should have brought my hair-drier!' she mourned as she entered the lounge, hair towel-wrapped turban-style.

'Allow me!' Cameron unwound the towel and gentled her to the carpet in front of his seat, opening his legs so she could sit between them. It was the obvious position but she felt tense, too aware of his thigh and calf muscles taut against his faded blue jeans, the length of his legs casually holding her.

'Comfortable?'

She wondered if anyone asked a mountaineer struggling up an almost sheer rock-face the same question.

'The others are looking after dinner. I gather the dishes will be our task.' He began to rub the towel against her hair, his long fingers firm and deft, the brisk movements impersonal, drying the overall scalp area. She began to relax, leaning against him, finding the comfort of his body supportive. 'Close your eyes, Catriona,' he instructed. 'Trust me, you'll find it pleasurable.'

It seemed churlish to question, natural to acquiesce; with her eyes shut her thoughts blanked to a dream-like state. Contentedly soporific, she enjoyed the deep, massaging effect on her head, her breathing deepened, and his movements slowed in time; at some stage she knew he had discarded the dampened towel, but his hands continued to lift and strand the hair between his fingers in a rhythmic pattern. It felt so wonderful that she snuggled against him, hoping the massage would go on, his circling fingers finding and relieving tension not only on her head but around her shoulders and the top of her spine until she was a floppy doll, completely relaxed. Gradually the pattern changed subtly, his fingers still stroking but their message caressing, then, as she could not resist, deepening the movement, his thumbs finding erotic pin-points around her ears.

'Mmm, your hair is a...a tangle of temptation.' He buried his face in it and she felt the sexuality charge through him as his fingers tightened over the contours of her shoulders. Sensually alert, she waited, forcing herself to be still, desperate not to show her body had quickened to his touch. With slow, rhythmic circular movements his fingertips searched and found and excited delicate nerve-ends under her jaw and behind her earlobes, wrenching response from her in a swift gasp of desire. His mouth tantalised her left ear. She was unable as well as unwilling to move away, but a remnant of control helped her to protest. He kissed her earlobe again, then, voice deep, murmured, 'I could make love to the Titanium Tigress, but would that destroy Snow White?'

The question throbbed between them.

'Catriona, you confuse me. You seem so innocent and sensitive; I want to protect you, yet I know the passion in you.'

'They are not incompatible.' She made the mistake of turning to look at him. The desire in his eyes was naked. Trembling, she sprang up, grabbing the towel like a protective shield.

'Catriona.' The way he said her name was a resonant poem, holding her with his eyes and his voice. 'Catriona...'

'I feel...torn, I...want you,' the words were dragged from her depths, 'but...instinct...upbringing...caution warn me. With you I'm afraid.' She looked into his eyes but the black pools held his secrets. 'How can I explain?' She moved away from him as if to distance herself, and, looking towards the dogs, trustingly asleep on the sheepskin, an incident replayed in her mind. 'When I was a child I used to visit a farm where there was an unbroken pony. Every day I talked to the pony, and held out choice titbits. Gradually he allowed me to venture closer to him, until finally I could feed him from my hand. From there it was easy to slip the bridle on.'

'The point being, you don't know me.'

'I know so little of you, apart from business. You made it brutally clear that work came first; now, because work has brought us together and you've some spare time, you torment me.'

'I torment you! You've plagued me for twenty-two nights.' He glared at her. 'I keep seeing those blue eyes of yours and that enchanting ruby mouth... I've made love to you a hundred times . . . and damned unsatisfying it was too!'

She could feel her smile grow at his admission and saw it reflected in the wry tenderness in Cameron's lips.

'Come on, dinner's ready!' The door was opened unceremoniously and the guide appeared. 'You sit over here, Miss Macarthur, and the boss at this end.' He gestured them to their seats and within a few minutes they were presented with bowls of venison soup, chunky with meat and vegetables.

'This is delicious!' Catriona said approvingly. 'A five-star hotel couldn't do as well.'

'Should be able to,' the guide sniffed. 'Easy enough. Used to make something like it in the old days. I had a restaurant then.'

'I imagine it was popular if the food was like this!' Cameron reached for a bread roll. 'Home-made?'

'Not exactly many bakeries in the bush. Besides, there's plenty of time.' He served the main course, the stuffed trout with lemon sauce, miniature barrel-shaped potatoes, fresh podded peas, beans and cauliflower. The home garden vegetables, like the trout, were just cooked to keep the full flavour. They ate appreciatively, the sauce of hunger and fresh air had given them an appetite.

'Most impressive! You're hiding your talents here.' Finished, Cameron put down his fork with a smile of satisfied pleasure.

'I wouldn't be alive if I were in town—too easy to get a drink. I'm an alcoholic. Here, I can't get the stuff and using the AA way I get by a day at a time.'

Hoping he would reassure the guide, Catriona looked towards Cameron. The ashen, taut lines of his face shocked her.

'Regardless of what plans we make, I'll give you my personal guarantee that this will remain a dry site as long as I'm chairman of Macarthur's.' He edged out his chair and stood up. 'Excuse me, I've work to do in my room.'

Trying to guess why Cameron had been so upset, Catriona gazed after him, aware his manner forbade interference with his privacy. The clue was in the guide's comment about alcohol. Frowning, she recalled Cameron's ridiculous accusations about Rory's occasional drinks. Had Cameron's father or mother been an alcoholic? Was that the reason why he had wandered the world's lumber camps and building sites after his university studies? Memory and reason told her it didn't fit. When Cameron had spoken about his parents he had been relaxed, smiling. His reaction to her first question about marriage when she had interviewed him in her father's study had been quite different. She had thought his upset due to natural grief. The personnel file had given only the brief fact, no reason for the tragedy. Could it have been that his wife was an alcoholic?

The guide slurped his tea and Catriona poured another cup for the pilot and herself. Suddenly aware of their speculation after Cameron's abrupt departure, Catriona made the effort to change their silent questions by mentioning the shining trout. Fishing was a favourite topic of both men and she was rewarded by their assistance with the dishes. Afterwards they sat and talked, but Cameron's continued seclusion in his room distressed her. With some hesitation she tapped on his door.

'Come in.'

She entered, taking in the fact that Cameron was surrounded by maps of the area and the bush reports she had studied earlier.

'You're working?'

'Trying to, Catriona.' He ran his left hand through his black hair in the gesture already familiar.

'Can we talk, Cameron? Maybe you're not ready to share the memory; maybe I run the risk of hurting you... You've not told me about your wife.' She saw the blinds pulled down in his eyes. 'I just want to help.'

'No.' He began piling the reports together.

She felt a chill at the depth of emotion in the single word but, certain of his anguish, she hesitated, sympathy convincing her to make one more attempt. 'As you wish. Just one comment I picked up somewhere: it's often the alcoholic's partner who needs the greater mental relief and counselling. Guilt, real or imagined, can be a heavy backpack.' She walked back towards the partially open door.

'How did you know Diane was...?' Unable to finish the question, his voice was a choked rasp, his eyes dark, agonised.

She spoke softly. 'Your reactions. Logic.'

He nodded, accepting the truth even as he turned to the window. For a time he stood, shoulders and neck hunched, arms forward, hands knuckle-fisted on the window-ledge, staring out to the blackness that was the lake. Catriona waited, hoping he would be able to confide in her. She longed to ask a dozen questions but compassion would not allow her to speak, his pain too evident. His voice was a dried reed. 'Diane was a poly-addict; that is, she was hooked on alcohol and drugs. She was twenty-three when she died. Until shortly before her death I never realised she was so afflicted. That will tell you about the sort of husband I was.'

Catriona realised with his last remark that Cameron was blaming himself for his wife's death. To help she had to know more. 'When did you meet Diane? At university?' she prompted.

'Yes. When we married two terms later I thought we knew each other very well; in fact, we had only shown our better sides. For the first few months life was idyllic, but the pretence and the romance eroded over the next two years. Shortage of money is hard on relationships. A lot of our friends after graduation began careers, but I'd decided to try for my masters. I don't think I ever realised how difficult it would be for Diane. She loved company and found studying difficult. We worked part-time to support ourselves but I was engrossed in my studies, committed to a research project, and our time off seldom coincided. Through my study I was offered a job part-time in the evenings. It suited my schedule, freed me for research work during the day and it paid well.' He stopped and moved back to the big window. A migration of moths beat themselves feverishly against the lighted glass.

'Diane and I discussed it; she didn't want me to do the shifts as she hated being on her own at night. I pointed out it would free her to study at the time I was away, and the money meant we could afford the books we required. And it was only four nights a week.' Cameron paused, reflective. 'I came up with a dozen reasons why I should take the job. It's easy to make moral justifications to suit a course of action.' His tone was embittered.

'And Diane was lonely?'

'Yes, several of our close friends had taken work down south. She missed them, and at first when she met up with a new group I was pleased. Until I realised they were more into parties than study, and it didn't help when I criticised them. We began having arguments. We had fights about money, about who did what in the house-keeping, about my time in study and work, about all the drink she was buying and the lack of money for decent food ... anything and everything. The truth is I was too selfish and too busy to help my own wife.' He walked with jerky movements back to the desk then re-traced his steps to the window. 'I kept thinking, only a few more weeks and it will be the holidays; we're both tired, irritable. We can sort things out then. Diane had begun skipping lectures and failing tests. She was drinking heavily and experimenting with drugs, and I didn't realise that either.'

Cameron walked restlessly to the chair but he did not sit.

'It wasn't obvious?'

'To everyone else; not to me.' His face was haggard. 'I had taken on two extra nights when Diane lost her part-time job. We saw even less of each other. When she told me the rent had gone up I began at five instead of six, so we didn't even have the evening meal together. The flat was close to the university so we decided it was better to pay up than shift. By chance I saw the landlord one day and found out Diane had lied about the rent increase. I was shattered ... I couldn't understand. Instead of going to the library I went home to see Diane. She wasn't there and I began tidying up the place, trying to work out why she'd lied. There were a couple of books Diane had needed and I picked one up to glance at it. She had told me it had cost thirty pounds but inside was the second-hand price of fifteen. While I was still looking at it Diane arrived home. She was drunk.'

Catriona said nothing, afraid that any comment would break the cobweb of his emotions.

'When I confronted her she said she was tired of being broke all the time and hated having to ask me for money any time she wanted to go out with a few friends or to have something new to wear. I was too furious to be tactful. When I'd calmed down I saw how unfair I'd been, leaving her alone so much. I decided to give up studying and get a full-time job. But when I told Diane she became almost hysterical. She convinced me that once we got through the next few months everything would be all right. It was the garbage I'd been feeding myself because, despite my long hours at work, I enjoyed my study and research. And I was tempted because I wanted my masters degree. So we kept on the cycle.'

One of the Labradors came into the room, looked at them, did a circle round Catriona's chair and then flopped mat-like at her feet. Absently she stroked its soft, short hair. 'And the holidays?'

'When the long holidays came I was offered a marvellous job in Norway in line with my research topic. I nearly turned it down but Diane persuaded me that if I could earn money in the holidays then I wouldn't have to work so many hours at night. And, of course, she knew I wanted to take the job. The topic was a bonus for my masters degree. When I reminded her that we had been intending to have time together to sort ourselves out she told me she had booked in for an addiction course, and when it was over she could stay with her parents.'

'So she admitted she had a problem? And you knew, too?'

'Yes and no. I guess I held too much of a stereotype image of a drunk in a gutter. And Diane wasn't like that. She went out, often to parties, but she was nearly always home before me. In the mornings her lectures started late so she was still in bed when I left at eight o'clock. I must have been blind and dumb not to see the pattern. By then she wanted me to work so she had the money and the freedom to get high without my seeing and interfering. If I had been at home she would not have been able to hide her addiction.'

'She was easy to live with?'

'No. I was a circus tightrope-walker before I walked in each day, wondering which mood she'd be in. But I made it worse because she knew I didn't want her sexually. I'm not sure how it happened; for so long she had treated me like a potential rapist. I'd moved into the spare room on the excuse I disturbed her when I came in from work at midnight and my alarm woke her at six each morning when I rose to study.'

'Alcohol and drugs diminish the sexual drive,' Catriona offered quietly. 'So do stress, lack of sleep and an inadequate diet. A period of holiday work apart would seem a heaven-sent chance to give yourselves time out.'

'That's more or less what we decided. I walked away, pleased to be out of it. The Norwegian forestry job was great, combining my research and technical skill with hard physical work; I'd forgotten how hungry it was possible to be and how food can taste so good after strenuous labour... I'd been struggling with my theories and arguments for my thesis, but suddenly it was all there. My boss saw the breakthrough and agreed with my ideas. Earlier he tried one of my suggestions and he estimated it would save the company thousands per year. He let me have an office where I could write my thesis and later arranged for an English-speaking secretary to type it up so I could polish and correct it. The encouragement was marvellous. I was so happy with my new friends that I didn't want to go home. Diane's letters were like black crows flying in occasionally to remind me that I had another existence. She wrote a little about the course and I persuaded myself that she was better on her own. When I was due home I went to the bank to draw out some money for a present. Part of the new start we'd written about. While I'd been working a small living allowance had been paid to me personally; the rest was direct credited. When the teller told me there were insufficient funds...'

'Joint account?' Catriona could have bitten her tongue for the unfortunate pun but Cameron was too upset to notice.

'The statement showed that Diane had taken the lot almost as soon as it was paid in. She hadn't even left me the fare home! I went back to my boss and asked to borrow enough for the ticket. He said the accountant had been slow in working out the bonuses, so I still had money to come. To this day I don't know whether that was a story or the truth, but the bonus was generous. I had a night travelling, which gave me time to cool down and rethink the situation. But all my fury and plans disappeared when I saw Diane. I couldn't believe how thin and strung out and yellow-pale she had become. Even her skin looked unhealthy. I remember thinking as I walked towards her that, if I hadn't known better, I would have taken her for a drug addict.'

Catriona bent to pat the dog to hide her own feelings. She wanted to put her arms around Cameron and just hold him, but the rest of the story had to be told.

'About three seconds later the jigsaw fell into place. All the lies, all the pretences, the voracious appetite for money. The addiction course had been a hoax. Possibly she had intended to go. She was so ill that she didn't care if I knew or not. I abused her family for not contacting me, but, of course, she had told them she was in Norway with me. I'd included an occasional postcard to her parents with my letters to her so she simply added a few lines and sent them on.'

Catriona nodded. 'Understandable.'

'We forced her to have counselling and I arranged for her to go to an addiction centre. But she needed twenty-four-hour a day watching. Some friends of mine and our families arranged a roster to be with her so that I could re-check my thesis and bibliography. It only took a couple of days but I felt guilty. When I handed it in Diane went with me. She seemed so much better that I began to think the problem had been exaggerated. As we walked back through the campus she reminded me of some of our happier times; we even had a coffee in our old seats in the café, celebrating that the thesis was completed. I never thought twice about it when she said she wanted to go to the toilet. I waited for her, but she didn't rejoin me. After a few minutes I remembered there were two exits. It was too late—she had disappeared. We searched for her but I didn't know where she went, or her source of supply. Four hours later a police officer told me Diane had been found dead in a derelict warehouse. She had been sold impure heroin and it had killed her.'

'Cameron, I'm so sorry.' Instinctively Catriona went forward and hugged him, wrapping her arms around him. It didn't matter about the tears dripping down her face.

It was a long time before either of them spoke. 'Poor, poor Diane. I'll say a prayer for her tonight. And one for you too,' Catriona comforted. 'You know, you've carried that guilt for long enough.'

'I'll carry it for the rest of my life.'

His statement tore at her. 'That would be wrong, Cameron. I'm not saying you should forget Diane; that would be impossible.' She sighed, picking her words with caution. 'You haven't discussed this with many, have you?'

'Not since the court appearance,' he admitted.

'A pity. You've walled up your emotions, shutting them away. I'm not an expert, but even I can see that you're blaming yourself for Diane's death.' She looked him in the eyes. 'Diane didn't intend to die. But she couldn't resist the addiction. That was the killer, along with the dealers and pushers.'

'But I left her to face that temptation.'

'Not knowingly. At the worst, you thought it was alcoholism in its early stages and that Diane was taking a course for it.'

'If I hadn't started night work...'

'Yes, you have a point, but that's all it is. Diane could have studied at the flat, realising that, although it was hard on her, it was worse for you. Lots of people have their partners working shifts or studying; they make allowances, even if they don't like it very much. And Diane knew it was just for a few months. Possibly she was bored, but she made a deliberate choice to go out to parties. There must have been students close by who would have been happy to study with her.'

'Yes, in the same building,' he admitted, 'but she thought they were dull company.'

There was another of the long silences while Cameron explored his conscience. 'I failed her in love.'

'That happens,' Catriona admitted. 'But it was not one-sided. If you'd been honest with each other from the beginning perhaps you might never have married.

But you tried to make it work. Even when you came back from Norway you were prepared to try again. But with Diane's addiction the best relationship wouldn't have stood a chance. If she had been able to overcome it you might have built a new trust together.'

Cameron was quiet, but there was none of the heavy atmosphere in the room. She felt his relief and comfort.

'You're exhausted, Cameron. Now go to bed and sleep peacefully.' She put her hand in his and brushed a kiss on his cheek. 'I'll say goodnight.' She left him alone, but her shoulders sagged and her eyes filled as she reached her own room.

The Labrador, following her, looked at her sympathetically, whining softly as the tears rolled down her face. But how could she explain to a dog that she was crying because Cameron had been so badly hurt that she doubted if he would ever be able to love again? And for her that was heartbreak, because she knew she loved the Black Scot.

CHAPTER SEVEN

'CATRIONA, what results did you get on the beech in section twenty?'

Catriona scrutinised her notes then played 'Chopsticks' on the calculator. She pulled a face when she saw the total.

'Well?'

'Even with our reserve and exigencies, it's within our profit line,' she admitted. 'These sections,' she fingered the map lying on the ground, 'are a write-off: shingle fans from the glacial moraine, and at higher altitude it has an area that could only make a cross-country ski-run!'

'Remember that next winter!'

Catriona felt herself warmed by Cameron's smile. She was aware of the change in their relationship, but the presence of the others had kept them professional for the first hour of work. Repacking her bag ready for the next check-point, she noticed the pilot and the guide were heading towards the craft.

'Catriona.'

Cameron's hand touched her fingers, but it was the gentle nuance in his voice which caused her to look up into his eyes. Joy leapt in her when she saw the dark shadows had gone.

'Until now there hasn't been the privacy to thank you, Catriona,' he said, voice low. 'But here, in this beautiful spot, I'd like to say I'm grateful for your courage and sensitivity last night. I'll never forget Diane but at least, now, I can live with her memory in peace.'

Catriona took his hand but said nothing, the moment having the delicacy of a moth's wing. She looked away from Cameron and knew he was following her glance, along the lakeside, across the floor of the valley, up to the snow-topped mountains.

'Oranga, the place of healing.'

'Yes.' Cameron's simple affirmative was enough.

Shattering the stillness, the start of the helicopter's motor and the increasing throb of the rotors broke the moment.

It was, Catriona considered several hours later, quite a remarkable day. At breakfast Cameron and the pilot had been cock-a-hoop, both having caught two trout, and the buoyant mood as the guide had set the fish to smoke, reserving substantial fillets for breakfast, had set the tone of the day. Then there had been the golden moment of shared understanding with Cameron, by the lake. But instead of the expected flight over the block Cameron had instructed the pilot to drop them into the bush, and he had taught her how to measure and analyse the sections. It had been hard work, with Cameron a thorough and painstaking teacher, but the discovery of how easily they understood each other was surprisingly stimulating. His knowledge and skill extended and impressed her. There was pleasure, too, in sensing Cameron's growing cognisance of her abilities, and mentally she gave a vote of thanks to Hemi for the sound preparation. She gathered her notes and asked the guide to pass them to Cameron.

'I thought checking the bush would involve little more than a helicopter ride. I've learnt heaps but am I exhausted!' She sighed gustily, then looked at him. 'We've redone parts of the block survey. Why, Cameron? Human resources are valuable!'

'As a director, you receive compilations of the forest section. In the past you've ignored them because you weren't informed. Hemi has taught you how to interpret the information, but the forest and the bush teach you what it means. From now on you'll look at a print-out and you'll read the quantities of timber expected from certain areas. You'll be seeing bush-clad slopes or forest flats and you'll be back in the bush...'

'Seeing the rata bloom fiery red and tasting the honeydew...'

'Fighting the wasps!' he retorted. 'You'll know what the staff do to assess a block because you've done it yourself, even if on a limited time-scale! There's another bonus too: Macarthur's have always had excellent relations with the union. Once you've worked in the bush you have an insight into the variety of problems encountered by staff. Instead of making decisions on the basis of apparent cost you'll be ready to listen when staff say they need equipment or they suggest alternatives. As far as I'm concerned the more directors who understand the roots and tree-trunks of the business, the better!'

'So instead of complaining I should be saying thank you!' She rubbed her leg muscles gingerly.

'I think it's been a profitable day, even if teaching you meant I missed out on some fishing. And you were a good pupil!'

She luxuriated in his praise. 'I think you just wanted an excuse to tramp in the bush and get your boots dirty!'

'Getting cheeky? That means we've done enough for one day.' He pulled out the radio and spoke to the pilot. The guide began piling their equipment together by the banks of the stream where the helicopter could land.

'Cameron, you just want to catch my giant trout!'

'He was a beauty! I hooked a big one this morning, but it spat the lure back out at me!'

'I wish I'd seen that!'

'You should have come with us instead of lying in bed, snoring!'

'I don't snore!' she exclaimed indignantly.

'I'd have to sleep with you to prove that statement.'

She laughed. 'Nice try, but no need. I've a tape-recorder I could set up if you're really interested.' The arrival of the helicopter broke the tender moment, but both were smiling as they were landed back at the cabin.

'No rain coming in—what about a barbie?' the guide suggested. 'I'll have the wood ready to a white glow by the time you land your fish.'

'That's a great idea—thanks! Coming, Catriona? We'll just fish from the jetty.'

She ran to join Cameron and he guided her tentative casting manoeuvres, chuckling with muffled mirth when she succeeded in snaring an overhanging branch. By the time they had rescued the line the pilot had caught a trout but had tossed it back as too small. The racing of Cameron's line made him leap back to his position, straddling a beam, and Catriona was happy to reel in her own line to clear the way. The tang of wood-smoke told them the barbecue was well lit. Half an hour later they were munching on the fresh trout. Between mouthfuls Cameron insisted on taking photographs and Catriona, laughing, extended her arms to show the size of 'the one that got away'. As she posed she dropped some food and squeaked in fright as a feathered object brushed her legs. She dived to Cameron's arms and he hugged her, then pointed to a pair of wekas which had decided to join their barbecue. Seeing the small brown hen-like birds was instant reassurance, but she made no effort to shift Cameron's arm from her waist.

'Feeding my prize to wekas!' he teased, his hazel eyes happy. 'Just as well there's another piece ready!' He reached over and, using the long-handled slide, dropped a piece on to her plate. 'Now don't give that to the kiwis!'

'Are there kiwis around here?' Catriona asked. 'A couple of times I've thought I've heard them but...'

'Go down two hundred yards past the first bend and there's a couple nested in a hole in the fallen kahikatea almost beside the track,' the guide informed her. 'Take a look. Course, you might have to wait a bit. The noise we've made might have upset them. But don't go alone! It'll be nearly dark soon.'

'Give me time to finish my dinner and I'll escort you, Catriona!' the pilot offered.

'No need!' Cameron's tone was silk covering steel. 'I'm interested in that verra special bird!'

'You're the boss!'

Catriona opened her blue eyes very wide and smiled innocently at the men. 'Why don't we all go?'

'They've got other things to do, Catriona,' Cameron drawled.

'Yes, I'd better get my report up to date,' the pilot agreed.

'I've seen those kiwis a dozen times,' the guide sniffed. 'And if they smell dog they'll stay put. The Labs need some attention.'

Catriona was still smiling as she helped Cameron wash the dishes. Finished, they put on jackets and, taking a torch, walked down the fern-encrusted track. In the gathering dark the bush seemed to listen, the subtle, silver sounds of the night so soft that their own trainer-clad footfalls were noisy. An occasional plop from the lake and the shrill whistle of a bird foraging were joined by the cro-ak of a couple of frogs. As though the first pair was the advance party, a regiment of frogs began croaking, the sound echoing across the lake.

'I think we could do a Highland reel down here and the kiwis wouldn't notice,' Cameron commented. He held out his hand and she slipped hers into his, the contact warming. 'While there's still a little light we should find a spot. There's the old kahikatea log,' he murmured, 'and if I'm not mistaken that dark patch almost hidden by the blechnum fern could be our couple's entrance.'

'If we stand here we'll be able to lean against this tree,' Catriona suggested. 'We're in the right direction for the wind; kiwis have an excellent sense of smell, even if their sight is poor.'

'We can do better.' Cameron pulled out a slim groundsheet and took off his thick bush jacket, opening it out and placing it on top. Noting that he wore another thick jersey, Catriona smiled but slid down. 'You must have been in the Scouts as a wee laddie.'

'Aye, and I helped women across the street and all.' He settled himself beside her, putting his left arm firmly around her waist and nestling her back against his body, supported by the tree. 'You always wear that intriguing scent . . . like a green wood with hints of citrus and some exotic flower and spice.' He nuzzled his mouth in her hair. 'It's just you . . . Some day I'm going to kiss your tiny toes and find your perfume there too . . . but tonight . . .'

Catriona felt his hands pull her round so that she was almost facing him, then he ran his finger around the outline of her face. 'So beautiful . . .'

She could smell the clean, warm smell of him; male, wood-smoke, fern and subtle aftershave mingled in her nostrils as she lay waiting for his kiss. His closeness sent sweet sensations through her, and when his lips hovered, then brushed hers, she was aching for his touch. She raised her arms around him, holding him, her fingers lifting his jersey and enjoying the tactile pleasure of his back, the smooth polish of his skin, one finger pausing to worry a small scar on his shoulder.

'A tumble when I was a lad,' he murmured, 'trying to climb the garage roof.'

'Why climb a roof?'

'Must you know all my wicked past, woman?' His eyes were tender. 'My brother had a new car and he had promised to show it off to his girl first. I never liked being second.' He looked at her solemnly. 'If you go down to my buttocks you'll find another, larger scar I collected at the same time.'

'I think I can only cope with one revelation at a time,' she murmured, blue eyes dancing. 'We came out to watch the kiwis.'

'Exactly! And I'm paying very close attention to my kiwi,' he murmured, 'and I can't resist her kissable mouth any longer...' His lips took hers; deceptively gentle, they were firm and knowing, responding to her quickened breath, his tongue seeking, exploring. His hands moved to caress, but in a self-protective move she held them back before he wrecked her control.

'Under the stars can be a very romantic place to make love,' he whispered, his breath churned by emotion.

It was an effort to look at the sky. 'I can't see any stars.'

'There might be clouds in the sky, but look...' He lifted a line of ferns covering the edge of the track. A thousand jewelled lights crystalled and spun in the dark, recessed area.

'Glow worms!' Catriona breathed. 'Cameron, they're magical.'

'There will always be stars for you, my beautiful Catriona.'

Again he held her close, his kiss a sweeet seduction. Heartbeat racing, her surging sexuality almost overcame the insistent nag of caution. She sat up, forcing herself away from Cameron, her limbs liquid.

'You want to be with me.' Cameron's voice was an ache in her ear.

She nodded, affirming the statement, then spoke urgently in contradiction. 'No, I mean no!'

He trailed his fourth finger slowly in circles against her ear and she trembled, her body giving away the powerful chemistry between them. She was unwilling to face the question in his eyes but she had to be honest. 'It's no good,' she admitted. 'You've only to touch me and I want you...but having sex with you wouldn't be right. I don't know if I can explain...' Her blue eyes were large and luminous. 'I suppose it sounds old-fashioned to say I want to be loved...' her earlier doubt became gloriously certain conviction '...but that is what I want. I want to love my man and know he loves me.' She shook her head and the black curls shone as they tumbled and jostled. 'Not short-term sex.'

Cameron released a tendril of her hair wound round his fingers. 'Love! I gave up on love a long time ago.' He reached down and picked up two leaves. 'See these? One just fresh and bright green—that was me when I fell in love. Now look at this one. It's only a skeletal structure; brown threads of cells are all that's left—it's given almost all that it was.' He handed her the brown one. 'Don't ask for love, Catriona. Never trust love. It uses its fools, making them grasping, deceitful, dishonest and despairing failures.'

She could have wept at his bleak, embittered expression. His guilt had been offloaded but he bore the marks, his emotions raw. 'But at its best?'

There was a silence. 'It sets aside rational judgement. There always seems one who gives and one who takes.'

'I disagree.' She spoke softly but with sincere belief. 'Loving is sharing, understanding, tolerating ... enhancing the individual.'

'Don't you think I reminded myself that a thousand times?' His mouth twisted as he savaged the green leaf.

She put her arms around him and laid her head against his chest. 'You're so hurt ... but you have to start trusting in love again, Cameron.'

'Little romantic! When you drop those rose-coloured spectacles you and I could enjoy each other without the hassle of futile emotions.'

'How can you say that?'

She gasped as, to prove his point, he pulled her down and in a swift movement rolled over to cover her body with his own, his weight pinning her against the fern and lumps of the forest floor. Before her breath returned she felt his lips against hers, stealthily stopping the protest by gentle persuasion, kissing her, his action firm and determined. In spite of her earlier statements, she found herself unable to think beyond the physical pleasure, the tactile sensations. 'You want me.' His voice was thick with passion. 'Love isn't necessary. Of course, I'll take care of you, I'll take precautions.'

'Physical but not moral ones?' She was surprised at her own lack of anger. 'And what if I say yes? What if I fall in love with you?'

From the stillness in his body she could sense his shock. Seconds later he rolled away and sat up, knees bent, long arms wrapped around his legs, his head down, locked into another world. She lay on the groundsheet, apparently quiescent, but inwardly forcing herself not to move, her hopes rising as his silent debate lengthened. For herself, she knew it was already too late. She did love him. But she would not accept him as an emotional blank tape. He had to be able to accept her love and be capable of giving love again. And the process had already begun. He had trusted her with his past, shown her his shattered dreams, his vulnerability and his bitterness.

'No! I'm not prepared to put you through that.'

She sat up and, reaching over, she kissed him, grateful for his answer. He was a man worth loving!

'I don't understand you! You sit there like Mona Lisa with stars in your eyes.' He studied her and she was afraid he would discover the truth.

A sharp distinctive 'Ki-wi-weee, ki-wi' sound, high and shrill, startled her. She could tell by the stiffening of his atttiude that he had recognised the call. They watched as the two grey shadows mottled with dark brown came closer, and Catriona took Cameron's hand in excitement as a third shape, a soft, small, dark tennis ball with long legs joined the larger birds. It seemed to bounce along, already using its long curved beak a fraction above the ground, scenting and finding minute grubs and insects. A piece of rotten log came in for special scrutiny by the kiwis and in between uttering their calls they excitedly chomped their way through a spider nursery.

'I don't think I've seen a baby kiwi before! It's so cute! The adults are larger than I remembered, though,' Catriona whispered. 'The last I saw were not much bigger than a hen. Their feathers look much softer, too.'

'You're looking at Apteryx haasti, the great spotted kiwi. You probably saw Apteryx australis, the brown kiwi.' She glanced at Cameron, surprised by his knowledge. His mouth twisted in a white smile. 'I told you I was interested in kiwis!'

Their muted chuckles were enough to startle the birds, which scampered over the forest floor with surprising rapidity, disappearing behind a screen of ferns.

'We were lucky!' Cameron hoisted her to her feet, then, while she re-rolled the groundsheet, he picked up the jacket. Switching on the torch, he held out a hand to her and together they retraced their way back to the bush cabin.

'Here's where we rejoin the world.'

She felt Cameron tousle her hair as though reluctant to finish the evening, but she noticed him straightening his shoulders as he opened the door. Inside, the guide and the pilot were playing cards.

'Was the forecast still for heavy rain tomorrow night?' Cameron asked the guide. 'Yes? Then we will plan to leave Oranga by three o'clock but depart earlier if we think it necessary.' He glanced at the pilot and Catriona. 'Understand?'

Nodding compliance, Catriona patted the two Labradors vying for her attention. It was safer than revealing her intense disappointment. The knowledge that Cameron was taking precautionary measures to make sure they could leave made sense, but bitter nonsense of her own desire to love him. In the office he was controlled, competent, confident; Oranga had stripped him of his façade, but he needed more time to rebuild.

'I hope it buckets down tomorrow morning, and high winds too!' she murmured to the dogs. 'In fact, I think it would be rather good if we could order up a decent

storm, keeping us here for a couple of weeks!' The
Labradors golden-eyed her in perfect understanding.

As the alarm clock beside her began its loud ring
Catriona knew by the birdsong that her wish had not
been granted. Disappointed, she showered and dressed
and went towards the kitchen.

'Good morning! A cup of tea?' Her heart lifted when
Cameron smiled at her. 'A perfect day!' he commented.
'You'll be back in Wellington tonight, Catriona.'

'You needn't sound so pleased! I like it here!'

The guide thumped the fishing box down by the door.
Catriona felt sympathy for the man; his job necessitated
his escorting them, yet his love for the wilderness was
making him feel a traitor. Before she left she would have
to tell him that she, at least, would be fighting to keep
the area unmilled. She frowned, wondering just when
and how she had come to the decision. It wasn't logical
to make decisions on emotions. If the reports showed a
profit line she had a duty to the company and the shareholders. She could imagine Cameron's and her father's
blistering scorn if she told them she voted against milling
because it would destroy so much beauty, a special environment of water, mountain and bush and birds. For
her that was of great value. Would the directors listen?
How many had glanced at the files and not bothered to
visit Oranga? Was that so surprising? If it had not been
for Cameron's insistence would she have even read the
files? How far would she be prepared to take the issue?
To a special meeting of the shareholders? She had a large
enough sized vote to force a meeting, but such an action
could damage the company. Which directors would side
with her? Her mother, Hemi and who else? Her father?

Cameron? Was it fair to involve him when, as chairman, he had a special duty?

'Catriona, come on, we're waiting and so are the trout!'

She snapped back into reality, hastily swallowing the rest of her tea, pulling a face when she found it had gone cold.

The pilot caught the first large fish and then they extended their lines again. Catriona hauled in hers when Cameron's reel whirred. She was quite happy to look around her; she needed to think, and she could only hope that the trout would keep Cameron occupied for sufficient time.

Again her gaze went to the stands of totara on the far side of the lake. They were due to check it after breakfast. But she already knew the value from the reports she had studied so closely with Hemi. The red-heart totara was the gold to make the bushmen and the shareholders happy.

Was there a profitable scheme to save the bush yet provide work for the bushmen? An alternative? Could she set up guided tours for trampers and fishermen? But there were plenty of such places eager for the recreational dollar, and the block was so isolated, so cut off from the natural wonders of the west coast. The isolation had saved it a hundred years before. But, in the age of helicopters, bulldozers and chainsaws, isolation was a nuisance, not a deterrent for milling.

'A beauty! Best I've caught!' Cameron's joyful shout broke into her thoughts. 'The fish fight to get on the line. It's like paradise!'

'A pity you can't keep it so!' the guide put in, and Catriona silently agreed. But the reminder had taken the joy from Cameron.

'Right, we'd better get cracking—we've work to do!'

As the guide started the boat's motor she pulled her jacket up to the neck, but the cold wind rushed against her face, making her eyes water. Even colder was the prospect that her vote would alienate the warmth and affection she felt growing with Cameron. Mightn't losing his respect mean the loss of the chance for winning his love?

'Something wrong, Catriona?' Cameron touched her shoulder as they landed. His sense of her emotions pierced her but she didn't trust him enough to reveal her thoughts.

'I don't want to go back,' she prevaricated. 'At least, not just yet. Another week here, being indulgently slothful, would be wonderful!'

'With you, here, I'd be more likely to be guilty of one of the other deadly sins!' He fluffed her hair.

'Envy of my fishing,' she looked up at him mock innocently, 'or greed with so much good cooking?'

'Anger at wasting my fishing time!' He laughed, equal to the challenge, as he handed over the fish to the guide. 'I'd like to take it back with me.'

After breakfast they resumed their seats in the boat to jet across to the far side. Cameron and the guide pulled the boat up on to the bank and Catriona stepped out on a fallen log.

Away from the lake the forest enclosed them, and to Catriona it seemed unfriendly, as though waiting in judgement.

'There's no birdsong!' she commented.

'The boat's noise. Give it a few moments and the birds will know we are not a threat—at least, not at the moment,' Cameron added. His soft whistle of appreciation as he studied the trees in front of them stopped Catriona's answer.

She, too, stood still, amazed at the sheer clean lines of the enormous tree. 'I've seen big trees before, but this is impressive!'

'From the approach I saw even bigger ones further back.' Cameron put on his equipment and turned to the guide. 'The easiest way to follow the stream?'

Catriona followed the guide as he tramped alongside the creek. Lianes and creepers in a giant's cobweb entrapped them, and in places they had to scramble in the stream and in others to slash their pathway clear.

'The forests of Gondwanaland.' Cameron held back a branch. 'Untouched by animals, isolated for millions of years after the collapse of the land bridges.'

Catriona wondered if the point could stop the milling.

'Have you noticed there are not the sphagnum moss curtains that grow in the fiordland bush?' Cameron gestured. 'Not the rain here.'

'Yes, you're right. I remember walking the Milford track and the bush here is ... Ouch!' She had made the mistake of looking around and walked straight into a snare of bush-lawyer.

'Stay still, Catriona, I'll free you in a minute. Just as well you wore that body-suit.' Cameron pulled out secateurs and began cutting through the long, rapacious ramblers until she was left with two pieces hooked into her hair. 'Sorry, darling, I think I'll have to cut a couple of curls. If I try to untangle it I'll make it worse.'

She would have let him shear off every curl if it had meant his calling her 'darling' in such a tender way. 'Whatever you think, Cameron.'

'Such demureness! Are you sure you're all right?' His eyes were teasing. 'That's one down, and here's the last.' He ruffled her hair. 'The rape of two locks!'

She looked up at him, her fingers automatically stranding the shortened curls.

'You're still beautiful!' He smiled and reached down to kiss her but, as though he was remembering, the touch was feather-light. 'You are too much temptation, woman!'

'Good!' She looked up at him and offered her lips, knowing she was demolishing his resolve when she slipped her arms around him. She felt his lips tease hers, then the sweet pressure as he kissed her, passion flaring between them. It was a shock when he picked her up and put her a few steps forward on the path.

'You are not, Catriona, repeat, *not* going to fantasise a natural physical urge! Come on, we've work to do!' He glanced along the stream where the guide had already disappeared. 'I'll go ahead; shout if you need me.'

She eyed him, wicked lights sparkling. 'You mean, if I imagine myself in love, Cameron?'

He snorted and stormed off along the path, then had to come charging back for his bag of gear. Handing it to him, she puckered her lips and blew him a kiss, delighting in his rueful expression. She was winning the battle; all she needed was a storm!

Apart from a brief break for a warming cup from the Thermos, they worked efficiently, Catriona's intelligence helping her understand the problems and pitfalls. Her hopes rose when she heard the faint rustle of the tops, which warned of a wind shift. Cameron glanced skywards too. 'Let's go! We can't risk being stranded at Oranga!'

Disappointed, Catriona returned with them to the boat. In haste they returned to the bush lodge, grabbed their bags and said their farewells to the guide. Catriona, reading his anxious eyes, could not leave without trying to reassure him. 'I'm grateful for your help. I want to tell you that I'll be doing my best to turn aside plans for milling. This is a special place—it is Oranga! I think the environment and the ecology of the region is very important. I've seen it, so I understand, but the other directors haven't. If you can think of any evidence or alternative use which would support protection I'd like to include it in my presentation to the board.'

'Thanks!' The guide moved, shifting his shoulders, awkward with emotion. 'You'll think of something! I've watched you. No one pushes you around, even the big feller! You're a gutsy woman! If you say it won't be milled then it won't be! Come down any time, you hear? That trout of yours is still waiting!'

'Miss Macarthur is being indiscreet and most unwise,' Cameron interrupted them, anger revealed in his dark eyes, tightened lips and tense stance. Control showed in the low drawl of his voice, making his words weapons. 'The remaining directors need more than an appreciation of beauty and a few trout to take to the shareholders.'

Blue eyes bright, jaw set, Catriona faced him. 'Cameron, I know that as chairman you have a duty to your position. As a member of the board I feel quite within my rights to give my judgement to our guide, who has been so helpful and who, having lived here so long, deserves more than ordinary consideration. I'm sure I can rely on his confidence.'

'Judgement should be based on facts not emotive female claptrap.'

'Emotive, female…I don't believe I'm hearing this…'

'Believe it! Now climb aboard the helicopter. I've no wish to be delayed here with you.'

'Why? Because you might find you have feelings after all?'

'I'm not going to trade words at such a petty level.'

Catriona, realising that his temper was fraying, dared him silently with her blue eyes, tossing her black hair in defiance.

'Get on that chopper!' Losing control, his voice blasted her like the sudden jet-thrust of a powerful engine.

'There's no need to descend to the kindergarten level of shouting at me!' She picked up her bag, shook hands with the guide and walked with deliberate dignity to the open door.

She had made Cameron lose his temper while she had kept hers. So why did she feel defeated? Had she won the battle but lost the war?

CHAPTER EIGHT

'RORY! What are you doing in Wellington?' Catriona threw her arms around her brother. 'It's so good to see you!'

'You look great, Pusscat!' He cast a glance round the apartment and saw the files on her large desk. 'Working? I might have known! Come on, switch off the computer. We're going out.'

'I shouldn't really—I've got a fight on my hands.'

'You too? Who's daring to take you on? What's it about?'

'I want to stop a bush block from being milled. Primeval forest, lake and mountains. But the statistics are not on my side.'

'The place of healing? Cameron said it was beautiful.'

She spun round, surprised. 'Cameron said that? But he's the one I'm going to have to fight!'

'Like brother like sister! If the dollar signs are against you, Pusscat, you might as well give up now!' He managed a deprecating smile. 'I'll dump my bags and then I'll take you out. C'mon, Catriona.'

'You're impossible! But I do love you. I've missed you, Rory. Give me five minutes to change.'

'Take ten! I have to watch my image!' He laughed. 'I've been told about one place that's supposed to be good. I'll ring and book a table.'

When she returned she handed her brother her car key, knowing he enjoyed driving her Ferrari.

'Cameron didn't tell you? Lost my licence.' He gave back the key. 'Bit of a nuisance, but I cope. The girls have to take me out now!'

'Rory, what happened? That machine of yours just begs to go over the limit.' She drove the car up to the street.

'I was the one over the limit,' he admitted. 'We'd had a bit of a party and I was flagged down. Useless lawyer couldn't get me off.'

'I should hope not! If you'd been drinking you would have been a menace on the road. I thought you had more intelligence.'

'Don't lecture me. I had enough to cope with from Cameron.'

'Cameron?'

'He shredded me. Only my clothes held me together! But let's go!'

Catriona frowned but, as she did not want to discuss the matter while driving in busy traffic, she waited till they were seated at the table and had ordered their meal. 'I'm confused. You and Cameron had a fight, yet you've come running to me. Do I get to wipe up the blood on the carpet?'

'What a nasty, suspicious mind you have, Pusscat! You're right,' he pulled a face, 'but wait until later.' Signalling the wine waiter, he spent some time in a discussion about the wines. 'By the way, you know you're paying!' Rory grinned.

'Broke again! Rory, you're incorrigible. It's just as well you've finished varsity and are able to work full-time. Your results will be out soon.'

'Two more weeks, but I'm not expecting good news... It's such a bore.'

'A bore? Rory, I don't understand.'

'That's what Dad said too... You're very like him.'

'You are diverting the conversation. I want some answers. Why did Cameron shred you, as you put it?'

'He has a hang-up about a few drinks. I was on a bit of a high at work a couple of weeks back. Cameron wanted to see me at the time. The office staff usually cover for me but I blew it. Cameron acted as if I'd stolen the greenstone taonga from the museum. Among other things he said he'd fire me if it happened once more.' Rory picked up the fine glass flute and drank. 'Today the impossible happened. The son and heir got fired from Macarthur's.'

'What?' Her mouth opened and her blue eyes widened in shock.

'I'm a free man! No more——'

'Are you telling me Cameron sacked you?'

Rory nodded.

'I don't believe I'm hearing this...it's crazy... impossible.' Her voice was a low murmur of disbelief.

'If you'd heard Cameron you would have believed it.' Rory pulled a face at the memory.

His expression convinced her and she began to realise the implications. 'Dad! He'll be devastated!'

'Pusscat, I need your help.' Rory's entreaty pierced her. 'You know Dad and Mum are in Los Angeles. Would you ring Dad and tell him? I couldn't do it. And I can't ask Mum to tell him either.' The troubled-boy smile tugged at her emotions, but the thought of her father's dreams being smashed and the preposterousness of Cameron's action for once took precedence. There had to be something she could do, something she could say to persuade Cameron to give Rory another chance.

'Hopefully Dad will never know.' She signalled the watchful waiter. 'Come on, Rory, we're going to Christchurch. Tonight!'

'But we're about to start dinner...!'

'Forget it!' She was already signing the docket. 'I couldn't eat and you don't deserve it!'

'I'm not going back, Pusscat!'

Ignoring his protest, she drove him back to the apartment, then checked her flight timetable. 'It's ridiculous. In a couple of years you'll virtually control the company. Cameron has to change his mind.' She stalked round her bedroom, throwing items into an overnight bag. 'I thought you were friends.'

'You're wasting your time! Cameron's reinforced steel where the job's concerned.'

'Rory, we have to sort this out before Mum and Dad hear.'

'Don't ask me to go back. It's been like a...'

He looked as if he was about to break down, and she hugged him in sudden sympathy. 'All right, stay here. I'll go.' Distressed, she pulled out her wallet. 'You'd better have some money. I'll write you a cheque too.' She signed one and left it on the table. 'I'll just make the late flight!'

An hour and a half later she instructed the taxi driver to stop at the Macarthur building. Despite her watch showing ten o'clock, the lights in the chairman's office were shining. She arranged for her bag to be sent to the house and, armed with her keys, let herself into the silent building. The lift hummed while the floor lights numbered in red flashes, and she straightened her back as the door swished open to the chairman's foyer. Her grandfather's and great-grandfather's portraits, visible through the glass doors of the boardroom, hurt her—

she had forgotten the redecoration. A gap on the wall awaited the portrait being painted of Sir James, and she supposed that one day there would be a picture of Cameron. But would there ever be a portrait of Rory? Had Cameron been wanting an excuse to fire Rory before he became a threat?

'Good evening, Catriona. I've been expecting you.' Cameron was standing at his doorway.

'You knew I'd come?' She looked at him, noting his tiredness. The drawn lines on his face punctured her anger in the same way that a pin burst a balloon.

'It didn't take a lot of deduction. The chauffeur mentioned he'd taken Rory to the airport for a Wellington flight.' He gestured her to a seat. 'I'm the big, bad wolf, right?'

'Yes.' She wished he hadn't sat down beside her.

'So, Catriona, let's hear your arguments. I presume you want Rory reinstated?'

'I'd like to hear your side first.'

Cameron raised his eyebrows. 'You do learn fast!'

'Don't patronise me, Cameron. I'm as tired as you and twice as upset.'

'Sorry, I've been imagining you racing in here, accusations blazing like a film cowboy's guns. You always surprise me, Catriona.' He reached for a file and handed it to her. 'It's all there.'

Catriona took it and settled to read, while Cameron went to his coffee machine and poured two cups. There was silence, apart from the rustle of paper. Mechanically Catriona thanked Cameron for the drink but she left it untouched, her mind too occupied by the evidence. At first she felt fury with the section heads who had recorded samples of Rory's errors, but it was the increasingly frequent comments on his mood swings and

disruptive behaviour which alarmed her, preparing her
for the revelation of the last few reports.

'Dope! Rory's on drugs!' She whispered the words,
not wanting to recognise the truth. 'And alcohol!' She
looked towards Cameron but he stood with his back to
her, gazing out of the window. Hearing her cry, he turned
and opened his arms for her. She ran to him, letting him
warm and cosset her, his silent understanding and
strength helping her to recover from the shock.

'Cameron, what are we going to do?' Catching his
expression unprepared, she saw the bleak shadows of
pain in his face. Suddenly realising the trauma and hurt
Cameron was reliving, she was furious with her brother.
'Cameron, I'm sorry!'

Hazel eyes looked down at her with a tired smile. 'I'm
all right. I was worried about you.' Cameron's hands
stroked her back, gently comforting. 'But the one we
should worry about is Rory.'

'I find it so difficult to believe,' Catriona murmured.
'Why?' The question was a plea for help. 'Why didn't
someone tell me?' She broke away from Cameron to pick
up the file she had dropped.

'Who wants to be the bearer of bad news?' Cameron
shoved his hands into his pockets. 'And who wants to
sack the boss's son? Those section heads know Rory's
trust shareholding. And they don't want to lose their
positions.'

She made an indignant protest.

'Tell me, Catriona, on the plane down here didn't the
thought enter your mind that, if I didn't rescind my
order, as soon as Rory had his shares you'd try to persuade a couple of other directors to vote with you to fire
me?'

Catriona felt the hot blush in her cheeks. 'It was only my initial anger,' she said, shamefaced. 'It made me realise there must have been more to it than Rory mentioned.' She opened the file again. 'If only I'd been here! These reports wouldn't be quite so damning if they were not trying to make allowances for him!' She put the file back on the desk in a gesture of defeat. 'Anyone else would have been told to leave after the first week's fiasco. His work is a mess!'

'When he was working part-time the staff covered up his mistakes or laughed his clown-act away. But once he was here full-time his addiction became obvious.'

'He had everything going for him.' Stress showed as her voice dropped to a monotone. 'Everyone loves him. In a short time he'll be the major shareholder. What went wrong?'

'You've just said it, I believe. He thinks he can't escape the responsibility of the shareholding and he hates the office work. And I don't think he was able to tell anyone.'

Catriona searched Cameron's eyes for clarification. 'This is hard for you, Catriona; you've always loved and protected Rory. If he had a problem he talked to you and you dealt with it. But you've been away and Rory has been learning to sort things out for himself. Unfortunately he came up against what I call a flagpole problem; to solve it he would have had to cut against his own nature and his upbringing.' Cameron's hazel eyes were reflective. 'Everyone has some gift, Rory's is charm. That's a major liability, as well as an asset. He loves people, but he can't help using them. It's been so easy for him; his smile asks and receives. Fortunately it's tempered by his sense of care; talking to him, you soon find he knows every local staff member, their partner's names and in a lot of cases he's visited them in their homes. Even their problems he seems to hear about before anyone else. But ask him the price of pinus radiata and he'll be stumped. He's just not interested.' Cameron paused. 'He's trained as an accountant but he found he loathed desk work. But he was trapped, wasn't he?'

'Trapped? Why didn't he just say he didn't like it? There are other departments...'

'In Macarthur's?' Cameron's lips twisted. 'You're still putting your expectation ahead of Rory's own needs and wants.'

Catriona frowned at the unexpected charge, then slowly nodded, realising its truth. She had been brainwashed, and she had done a considerable amount of the soaping and scrubbing too.

'By the way, did you do an aptitude test before joining the firm?'

'Of course not. I worked here after school and varsity and, like Rory, I just moved into place when the holidays began.'

'Anyone else would have been sent to personnel for an aptitude test before they were hired. A pity Rory never did one; it could have saved him a lot of anxiety, and Sir James would have foreseen the possible outcome.'

'But Rory's not unintelligent.'

'Of course not! Look at his past university results; he achieved As and B pluses in psychology and sociology, but he's just passed economics and accounting and bombed in statistics. He should be doing arts or humanities, not struggling in commerce. He wanted to change but was talked out of it. A pity! This year he probably realises he's going to fail. You look astounded, Catriona. He loves you and, knowing your expectations, he couldn't tell you. And if he couldn't tell you, he certainly couldn't tell his parents.'

'So he started taking drugs and drinking?'

'It's guesswork, but it could be the reason.' Cameron put his hand on her shoulder. 'Feelings of inadequacy, fear of disapproval... his love for his family and their expectations... Rory's grown up knowing he was the next Macarthur of Macarthur's. That's a load to sling off when you're brought up to be the chairman of the family firm. And his favourite person, his beloved big sister, didn't make it any easier either. If she had said she wanted to study medicine or paint pictures perhaps the expectation for Rory might not have been so narrow. But, like a bright comet, she soared effortlessly into place.'

Catriona grimaced. 'I wouldn't have said effortlessly! But I do see your point. For me work is fascinating. It was taken for granted we would work here.' She frowned, struggling to accept the new scenario. 'What will happen? Rory will have his trust shareholding soon. He has to understand the policies and decisions.'

'Does he? The company directors have managed without him so far. Doesn't Rory have the right to choose his own career?'

'But...' She looked helplessly at Cameron.

'You've told me some of the difficulties you faced being a Macarthur. What is to one a goad is to another a load. How was Rory when you saw him? What was Rory's atttiude when he told you I'd fired him? Did he want you to come charging down here?'

'Of course, he expected me to...' She stopped, re-alising she was putting her own interpretation on the events. The black curls tumbled and jostled as she put her hands to her head, closing her eyes to re-visualise the scene in the restaurant. With Cameron's insight she was forced to re-interpret. 'No! You're right. He was

relieved! Although he was concerned about Mum's and
Dad's reaction. He told me I was wasting my time, that
you'd not change your mind.' Her blue eyes misted.
'Rory doesn't want you to reinstate him, does he? For
the first time he thinks he has a choice to do what he
wants. He said "I'm a free man!"' She looked at
Cameron. 'I didn't see his struggle. But you did.'

'I've been there, remember? No one made Diane face
up to her problems and I ignored them until it was too
late. You helped me come to terms with that, but I can't
forget. If Rory accepts counselling now he should be able
to sort his life out. He has to deal with his problems,
and begin with his addiction.' Cameron rubbed his
beardline in a slow action with his left hand. 'In the
future Rory may return, perhaps in personnel, legal or
welfare sections, but only when it's his choice and when
he's earned it. We can hire technical expertise, but im-
aginative capacity and charm is another ball-game. Come
on, Catriona. I'll drive you home. You look exhausted.'
He slipped his arm through hers and led the way to the
lift. 'Will you stay? There's the board meeting in three
days.'

'No, I'll get back to Rory. We need to talk and I'll
remember to listen to words he doesn't speak.' Her face
twisted in a sad smile. 'I've still got a battle at the board
meeting?'

'If you mean do I expect a reasoned, cogent set of
arguments not to mill Oranga you've got it exactly.'

She brushed a curl away from her eyes. 'I'm sending
out copies of the data tomorrow—correction, today.
Which reminds me, Mum and Dad will be back tomorrow. Can I ask you not to tell them you fired Rory
until I have a chance to talk with them?'

'Willingly! Perhaps now he knows that you understand Rory will have the strength to tell them himself. It would be better for him.'

She reached over and kissed him. 'Thanks for helping us, Cameron. You make it all seem so logical and simple. The main issue is Rory's health and happiness. While you're around the company will be in excellent hands.'

His smile warmed as he enfolded her. 'So long as I've you in my arms I couldn't give a damn for the company!' he murmured. 'You feel so good, so right...'

She leaned against him, enjoying the physical closeness and the good, clean smell of him, spiced with a tantalising hint of cologne. Leaning her head against his chest, she felt as if a burden had slid from her, and she sighed with satisfaction. 'I hadn't realised what a joy it is to have someone who cares and who can make hard decisions.' She smiled up at his hazel eyes. 'That doesn't mean I'm giving up my responsibilities... just that now and again I might trust your judgement.'

'I'm overwhelmed with your faith in me,' he teased. 'But I suppose it doesn't extend to sleeping with me?'

'We couldnt risk it. I'd be head over heels in love with you by morning. Besides, I wouldn't be satisfied with one night. I'm greedy—I definitely want marriage.' She peeped up at him, her blue eyes sparkling. 'To you! Think what fun we could have... every night, and quite legal!' She snuggled against him, nestling deliberately. 'I'm driving you crazy, aren't I? You want me so much... but you're afraid of love.' She hesitated, then spoke softly. 'Tonight I've learned something else—to communicate... to express feelings and wishes. So I'm going to say something more. Cameron, you decided never to marry again, didn't you? I want you to rethink your situation. Not for the company or your image, but for you and me!' Conscious of his rigidity, she reached up and arched her head, her black curls tumbling back as she moved to tempt him. With petal-tenderness she brushed her lips against his mouth until she heard the snap of his control with his groan. Her mouth opened, full-lipped, to his hunger, satiating and encouraging his demand.

'Catriona, you sexy female!' His voice choked with sensual torment, he forced her away, but she could feel in his hands his reluctance to release her. 'I'm not going to marry anyone!'

'Mr Chairman, amend the last statement.' She smiled. 'Anyone but Catriona Macarthur!'

'You're the last person I'd marry! Everyone would say I was after your money and shares!'

'Can't you do better than that? At least you could have said that they'd think you were besotted with my body!'

'Or your blue eyes? Or your black curls? Or your satin skin that tantalises my fingers?'

'That's more like it,' she smiled. 'Think about us! In the meantime I'd better go home.'

'Content that you've given me a few sleepless nights?'

'I hope so!' Her blue eyes smiled up at him through brushes of dark eyelashes.

'Don't do that to me!' He pushed his fingers through his hair.

'You like my smile?' she enquired. 'I'm pleased! It's nice to know one's advantages.'

He punched the lift button. 'Out! Now!'

It slid open obediently and he walked in beside her and hit the basement-level button. In silent harmony they walked across to the lone car in the basement.

'Dad has the chauffeur?'

'Of course, my little, wise one! Sir James found it difficult to manage without him! And Rory has kept him occupied while your parents are overseas.' Cameron started the motor and the car hummed into action.

In five minutes they had reached the portico shielding the front entrance. Not daring to risk his embrace again, Catriona leaned over and kissed him swiftly. 'Goodnight, sweet man!'

Seconds later the door opened for her and she was inside, her whole body trembling. Breathing deeply, she regained control, grateful that Cameron had not suspected how much she had been tempted. But, though she had been joking with him about marriage, she had meant every word! He was the right man for her, a man who attracted her physically, a man she respected and trusted, a man she found easy to communicate with and to understand. A man strong and mature enough to be gentle, one who would encourage her to grow to her potential. She pictured him laughing; she loved the way his mobile lips curved up and the sunshine lit his eyes . . . but would she ever see love in them?

The experiences he had suffered with Diane had made him wall away his emotions. He had meant it when he'd said he would never marry. She had recognised determination, even though she had laughed when amending his statement. He had built a castle of work where he could be secure. By forcing him to see the moat he had dug around himself had she lost her chance to surprise him? Wasn't it being unrealistic to expect him to build a bridge for her to cross? Or should she tempt him out by offering him something he wanted? Sex was not enough; she wanted his love, because she loved him.

*   *   *

'You have to consider the profitability of milling the block against the damage to the ecosystems.'

Catriona paused in her summary for the board of directors. Two vacant chairs marked the absence of her parents due to a delayed flight. She had hoped to talk her plans through with them, swaying them to her point of view before the meeting. Aware of Cameron's impatience, shown in the slight movement of his shoulders, she discarded her notes. 'I ask you to vote against the proposal. Oranga is an area of remarkable beauty. We cannot justify the gains against the loss.'

She stopped, realising she was becoming emotional. To be convincing she had to remain dispassionate. 'The scientists warn us of damage to the ozone layer. There is an increase of skin cancers. Burning and wastage of the forest and acid-rain pollution contribute to the greenhouse effect. Climate is creating new extremes, floods, deserts...' she saw one of the directors begin to fiddle with his papers and knew she was boring him '...but you are thinking that if I wanted to preach I should have gone into politics or the pulpit.' She leaned forward. 'Well, I believe it is up to each one of us to do whatever we can to help.'

'While I admire your youthful idealism, Miss Macarthur,' one of the directors put in as he glanced at his watch, 'altruism is hardly a motive the shareholders appreciate. And the grand old company is not about to waste a forest...its harvests.'

Catriona flinched. Help came from an unexpected quarter. 'Continue, Miss Macarthur; your report has been thorough and the points valid——' Cameron spoke firmly '—especially as you are one of the few directors who took the trouble to see the block in person.'

'Thank you, Mr Chairman. However, my fellow director has a point. So I'll be a realist! The potential profit figures are in front of you. Now on the debit column is another figure which almost exactly halves that profit. When I prepared the sheet I left out what that figure stood for.' All were looking at her, interest renewed. 'It's the projected costs of public relations for this company for the next four years while we mill the block.' She waited for the mutters of disbelief to settle. 'That's a conservative estimate. If we mill Oranga Macarthur's is going to call down upon itself the curse of the greenies; every politician in the country will use us as a whipping-boy; the media will have open slather. A few minutes ago I showed you the video our PR department prepared. Imagine a similar presentation on television accompanied by the news that Macarthur's was to clearfell! The outcry would rock those who voted to mill from their padded directors' chairs!' She let the words hurt. 'The annual general meeting? It would be taken over by the protestors! We, who have been admired for our policy on sustainable forests, for our coppicing programmes and our plantings on degraded land, make the bigget PR blunder of the century! Our share price would fall. We would lose many shareholders who invested their money because they want it to do good, as well as make a profit. Reading the signs, the speculators would dump their Macarthur shares, causing the market price to drop further, and in turn the investment-trust computers would ring alarm bells. Every single one of us stands to lose substantially if that occurs.' Seeing Cameron's frown, she knew she had won a major point. 'Wait! Let's reverse the situation. Keep the block intact. Our effort towards a better world! We set up the public-relations scoop of the year! We'll get free television, radio and

newspaper coverage, which will be worth millions to us.
Mr Chairman, fellow directors, I ask that you vote now
to save Oranga!'

She sank back into her chair, her hands trembling,
not daring to look again at the man at the head of the
table.

'Thank you, Miss Macarthur.' Cameron was formal
as he asked for any further discussion.

Catriona's hopes drooped as one of the workers' representatives produced figures for the creation of jobs by
milling the area. When Cameron looked at her to rebut
the argument she shook her head. Saving the bush would
possibly give work of a different kind in years to come,
but she had no figures to prove it.

'We will proceed with the vote.' Cameron outlined the
procedure. Catriona sat still when he asked for the call
to mill. As the hands went up she knew dismay.

'The motion is lost.'

Catriona felt her body sag. She had only two trumps
left, but using either would shock and hurt her parents.
Worse, she would alienate Cameron. The first would be
to ask for a special general meeting of all the shareholders. But to do so would be costly and time-
consuming—bad for the company, and she had no
guarantees that she would win. Reluctantly she took out
her last card. She would save Oranga but she would lose
Cameron, as well as her fortune.

But she had to stop Oranga being milled.

Her chair squeaked on the parquet flooring. Slowly
Catriona stood up. 'Mr. Chairman, I have another
proposition regarding the block, and before we proceed
I would like to present it. I believe it would save the
board time.' She waited for Cameron's nod. 'You have
the proposed maximum figures from milling the block.

I would like to offer that sum to purchase Oranga in my own right, my intention being to stop the area from being milled. My offer would have to be conditional upon the successful sale of most of my shareholding and a settlement date of three months.'

The startled gasps and buzz of comment interrupted but did not deter her. 'I have the papers here, and with the chairman's approval,' she saw the look of incredulity on Cameron's face, 'I will pass copies around for verification.'

Five minutes later she owned the block conditionally. A feeling of sadness threatened her, but she had to maintain her composure; she still had to tender her resignation as a director—she had no right to expect to remain once her holding had been sold. She tried to catch Cameron's glance but he was listening to the last report on the agenda under general business. He seemed to be deliberately looking past her, and when he asked for any further business in the closing routine she had to stand before he acknowledged her.

'Mr Chairman, as I will no longer be a major shareholder I wish to tender my resignation from the board of directors.'

'Miss Macarthur,' his frown revealed his displeasure, Catriona thought miserably, 'as you are the legal holder of the shares until the sale is registered through the stock exchange I will not consider the resignation at this stage. Therefore, I direct that the subject be held over until settlement.' He gazed around the room and then spoke quietly. 'If there is no other business I will close the meeting and thank you for your deliberations on behalf of Macarthur's, the grand old company.'

As the meeting broke up Catriona excused herself from the usual social time by using her parents' flight arrival.

She did not feel able to cope with casual questions about Rory or with offers for her shares. The chauffeur drove her to the airport in time to see the international flight land. There was a short delay before Sir James and his wife walked towards her.

'Catriona!' They engulfed her with their hugs and she felt her eyes mist at the thought of how quickly and keenly she was going to hurt them.

'It's good to see you!' Sir James smiled. 'We thought you'd be tied up at the meeting. First one I've missed in ten years! You can bring us up to date at home. How's Rory? I thought he might have met us. He usually makes us an excuse to knock off work!'

Catriona bent down to pick up one of her mother's bags, and the arrival of the chauffeur to assist with the rest diverted her parents' attention. By asking them questions about their journey and the sporting and youth foundations they had visited Catriona managed to keep them talking until the saloon stopped in front of their portico. Her mother glanced round the garden, scanning her beloved territory.

'There's no place like home,' Sir James announced as he followed his wife inside. 'I was beginning to think it must have fallen down. Now, Catriona, you've ascertained we are well, we are home, so tell us what's wrong.'

She had forgotten how easily her father read her thoughts. There was no delaying the news—at any minute they might be disturbed. 'You asked about Rory...' she began. While they listened to her account she felt crushed by their pain. She left them reading Rory's file, then went to the kitchen to order tea. When she returned her parents were sitting like children stunned into good behaviour. 'There's a letter Rory wrote to you. He's having treatment . . .' She broke off, handed the letter to her mother, then began pouring the tea.

When her parents had finished reading she had to tell them of her decision on Oranga. She ached at the thought, seeing their distress over Rory, but business calls over her shares would soon overwhelm them like a tsunami unless she forewarned them.

'There's something else you have to know, too. It's nothing in comparison, but . . . today at the meeting I tried to stop the milling of the bush block we gained in the Lumber South takeover. You've never seen it, but I hope you will soon. Milling would be a violation. Cameron and Hemi and one of the investment accountants voted with me, but the trust lawyers outvoted us. We lost! So I did what I thought was right. I made an offer to buy the block myself. It was accepted conditionally on the successful sale of most of my shares. After that I knew I had to resign, but Cameron deferred that until settlement in three months.' She saw her father's dismay. 'I've never even considered selling my shares before. They were untouchable. But I didn't have difficulty making my choice. I couldn't stand by and let Oranga be destroyed.'

Tears were running down her cheeks but they were not just for Rory and her parents. They were for the love she had never known, the chance of love she had destroyed by her action. Cameron would think time had revealed she was another scheming manipulator; a woman who, not getting her own way, had deceived him, using her money to buy what she wanted.

CHAPTER NINE

'As soon as we've helped Rory we'd better fly over and look at the block that's reduced our company's tiger to a wet kitten.' Her father's hug was comforting. 'Perhaps the trust and your mother and I could buy some of your shares... It's a pity that I've just sold some other investments to raise funds for the foundation. But you'll manage, Pusscat.' Her father's blue eyes held a smile. 'It's ironic, isn't it? We've been studying how to help other people's children and we didn't know our own son was becoming a poly-addict, and on the day we're told our daughter virtually gives away her shares in the family business.'

'Cameron did try to tell us about Rory.' Catriona's mother played with the rings on her hands. 'Several times. And we didn't want to know. If a plant doesn't do well in my garden I'll give it special attention, and if that doesn't work I'll dig it up carefully and replant it in a different situation. I don't try to make a rambler rose into a specimen tree, I enjoy it for its ability to climb and shower flowers. Yet I couldn't see such a simple truth with our son.' She stood up. 'I'm tired. All I want to do is to go to bed and sleep! Catriona, we'll talk more in the morning, but right now your father needs a rest too. Even if you see Dutch elm disease in my garden, don't dare to disturb us!'

After her parents had left the room Catriona walked out to the garden to ease the heartache of the day. She wandered along, unaware of the evening perfume of stocks and roses until she stumbled on a tree root snagging the carpet of lawn.

'Catriona! Are you all right? It was hard telling your parents?'

'Cameron! I wasn't expecting you.'

'Then you're not functioning as lucidly as you should be! In the circumstances that's understandable.' His smile softened his words.

'I'm fine now.' She hesitated. 'Actually I'm glad you came. I need to talk to you, to try to explain. From your attitude I thought you wanted to mill Oranga. Thinking I had to fight you, I prepared for the worst. I wanted to discuss with you the possibility of buying Oranga, but it would have meant placing you, as chairman, in a position of divided loyalty.'

'You had mentioned the possibility of calling a special shareholders' meeting.'

'It would have been bad for the company and worse for you.'

'Buying the block seemed a better option?' Cameron's expression was hidden by the shadows cast by the garden light, but she could tell by his voice that he was smiling. A sky-rocket of hope that Cameron had understood and believed her reasons flared.

'I had to save Oranga.'

'You are an incredible woman, Catriona Macarthur! I've never admired anyone so much. I'm verra proud to be your friend.'

Joy exploded into a thousand bright flowers of flame as she realised that Cameron had not only understood but was proud of her actions. She glowed at the thought of his admiration. And she had thought she had lost all chance of his love!

'Many talk, but when it comes to putting their money on the table it's often a lot of hot air.' He slipped his right arm around her waist, his hand reaching for hers. She leaned against him, realising how badly she had underestimated him.

'I've just realised a bonus in buying Oranga!' Her blue eyes flicked up at him, sparkling with humour. 'When we get married I'll know you wanted me for myself, not for my shares or money!'

'Catriona Macarthur! Don't you ever give up?' He stopped walking but he still held her hand.

'I have been known to waver,' she admitted, recalling her near-despair of a few minutes earlier. 'But determination and lateral thinking is part of the family tradition.'

'What do I have to say to convince you? I am not interested in matrimony. Do you want it in writing?'

'Save paper, save the trees! Just think, I am now the owner of a cabin by one of the best fishing spots in the country! Surely that must make me highly desirable?'

'There wasn't a question about your desirability.' His eyes darkened. 'You know how much I want you, Catriona.'

She shook her head and the black curls shone silver. 'Red-eyed and all?' she asked, her voice sad. 'Work brings us together but you've never gone out of your way to visit me or take me out. Time for me to stop joking, Cameron. I didn't mean to embarrass you.' Her sober demeanour was ruined by her making the mistake of letting him see laughter in her shaking shoulders.

'You're more dangerous when your claws are sheathed, tiger! Would you give me the pleasure of your company for dinner tonight?'

'How charming of you to ask!' Repaying his mock formality, she bowed, hands folded in front of her demurely. 'But regrettably I must decline. I've a flight back to Wellington at dawn.'

Cameron frowned. 'It's been cancelled. Tonight you are dining with me.'

She raised an eyebrow. 'I don't appreciate masterful men!'

'Tough! Besides, I want to see you in my office at eleven-thirty tomorrow morning. The Wellington manager has already been informed. My secretary left a message here.'

'In that case, I am your obedient servant.'

He uttered a sound between a yelp and a snort. 'I wish I had a tape-recorder here.'

'About dinner; can we have it here? The housekeeper prepared a welcome-home meal for Mum and Dad, but they were too upset and travel-tired to think about food. As for me, I'm not really in the mood for going out— it hasn't been the easiest of days.'

'Yes, of course. I'll take you out next time.' He laid his hands on her shoulders to turn her around so he could see her face in the neighbouring light. 'You are tired. Purple shadows under those magnificent eyes. Would you like me to leave you?'

'No, Cameron,' she pleaded. 'I really would like you to eat here. At the directors' lunch neither of us ate much. Now I know that the worst scenario happened I'm hungry,' she added with a grin, 'and I can guarantee no photographers! Now tell me why you want to see me in the office tomorrow. Otherwise I'll spend most of the night trying to work it out. The Wellington office has been buzzing with the rumours of reorganisation and streamlining.' She came to a halt. 'As I view it you're going to make me redundant or promote me!'

'Seeing you've worked that much out, I'll admit there is a new position for you. We've been studying the branches. Wellington has been under the microscope this time. In the past six months the figures per staff member have improved dramatically. I'm told the manager there has been following advice suggested by a certain Catriona Macarthur——' he ticked each off on his fingers '—team consulting, management organisation, and marketing. You've glided in and, like oil on an engine, you've slotted things together without clashes, identified and strengthened the weak links and always maintained a high output. What I found helpful was that while you were in Palmerston North and at the bush cabin the system carried on. The evidence convinced me you were the right person for a position I'm recreating. It means that you will be assisting me with the overall management. I want you as my deputy.'

'Deputy! Me?' She struggled to take in the implications.

'For once I believe I've surprised you!'

'Stunned would be the word! It's a plum position, Cameron.'

'Like all plums, it has a hard stone.' His voice was sober. 'I had to select someone who could not just do the job; I wanted someone who works creatively, consistently, a person able to hold an opinion of her own, whom I could respect—it's essential that we work well together—and preferably a person familiar with the company.' He shrugged his shoulders and his eyes held the familiar sunlight. 'When it came down to it you were the obvious choice!'

'I'm flattered, but I'm also uncertain.' She hesitated. 'Do you think it's wise to work together? I find you very attractive.'

'I've no objection to being seduced by you. I wish you had no objection to being seduced by me! But, as we both know where we stand, I think we can leap that particular hurdle.'

Catriona forbore saying that most hurdlers were running, not standing, when they made their leap. 'I'd like to study the other conditions of the appointment.'

'Spoken like Sir James! You'll earn more than double your present salary and bonuses, and you'll be a member of the staff share scheme at the highest level. Holiday leave as set out in the staff schedule and, as you'll be on transfer, you'll be eligible for housing loans at special rates from the company. For the rest, in my office, eleven-thirty.' He smiled. 'You could do with a sleep in! Now, what were you saying about dinner?'

Catriona put the pages of neat typing on to Cameron's desk. She had to make a decision about his offer. The work and the challenges offered would be stimulating and encouraging; the higher salary would mean she could afford to keep slightly more of her shareholding in the company. Shifting to Christchurch would allow her to sell her Wellington apartment and, with its prime site and luxury décor, she could ask a high price, which in turn meant selling fewer shares. Living at home would please her family, although she would miss her independence. She sighed gustily. The figures made such sense; her hesitation and uncertainty over the new position was nonsense. Most of the night she had lain awake, trying to make up her mind, but, like a revolving clock mechanism, when the offer swung one way then her emotions tugged her the other.

The silver pen was placed ready on the desk. Cameron had gone through the details of the position, then had left her to go to his next appointment. The work itself sounded absorbing, and the fact that Cameron was ready to delegate so much was evidence of his trust in her negotiating skills and business acumen. Glancing at her watch, she realised that Cameron was due back. If work as his deputy was the highest compliment he was able to offer, shouldn't she accept? What was the old proverb about half a loaf?

But could she withstand the daily turmoil in her emotions, the desire aroused by a man who had only to glance at her to make her aware of her own intense sensuality? Cameron had laughed about the risk; was his apparent immunity the thought which troubled her most? Yet if she threw away the chance to work with Cameron she would regret it for the rest of her career. Her ancestors might understand her buying land with her shares, but they wouldn't approve of her throwing away opportunities on an emotional whim!

She reached for the silver pen, then balanced it, her index finger on top, her right thumb sliding across the quality paper as she signed. With careful precision she centred the papers on his desk. The decision made, she straightened her shoulders and walked to the window. Her father and grandfather had plotted new strategies while staring from the same spot, across the river with its weeping willows, past the pines in the park, across the suburbs to the mountains in the distance. She felt herself begin to smile; parting with most of her shareholding would be a loss, but she had saved Oranga! In her new position she could begin to rebuild her financial base. Her emotions would just have to be kept under management techniques too!

Cameron's arrival surprised her. As she saw him her heart leapt like a flower in a gust of wind. 'I didn't hear the lift.'

'I use the stairs—part of my keep-fit programme this month!' He glanced at the papers on his desk and saw her signature. 'We'll be able to schedule some tennis games on the staff courts. I won't be satisfied until I beat you in straight sets!' He sobered, looking at her. 'Thank you for trusting me, Catriona. I'm sure we will enjoy working together.' He signed the document. 'You will have noticed your position starts in two weeks. It's not long and you have the right to extend the period, but I'd appreciate the early start. I need you here.' He smiled at her as he placed the contract in a file tray. 'After lunch I'll inform your boss in Wellington and Personnel can advertise your position there. Temporarily the staff can split your workload. If you need assistance in the transfer Personnel will have instructions to provide it. Any questions?'

'Not at the moment.'

'Fine; I've one for you. Have you given thought to the disposal of your shareholding?'

'Yes, of course. I'm still working out what I have to sell.'

'Stripping your assets?' His eyes teased. 'You look untouched. Can I assist?'

She smiled at his gibe but spoke with care. 'I want to keep as many shares as possible. The obvious way is to sell them in a block to an investment trust, but I've been thinking of selling them to a production company, one which can work with us to improve our value to raw product. At present we export such a lot of potential profit as logs or chip instead of processing it locally.'

She glanced at Cameron, waiting for his reaction. His slight nod told her to continue. 'Cost is always the factor; plant, labour and electricity. Macarthur's has the capital to set up a factory on the coast, and we could employ people rather than make them redundant. The electricity suppliers might be the key. Since deregulation the southern electricity companies have new goals and plenty of hydro-power. If we combined to form a subsidiary company we should be able to make it a profitable concern.' She stopped speaking, aware of Cameron's admiring grin. 'It's only an idea! It needs research.'

'I'm glad you're on my side, Catriona!' He pressed the intercom and ordered his secretary to send in the head of the research and development office. 'We haven't much time to negotiate the best price and the best solution for the company. Your shareholding would possibly carry two directors within the constitution.'

'You can have my resignation any time.'

'No, I want you on the board,' he smiled. 'You remember those old documents we looked at? I took the time to go through most of them. In your grandfather's time there was a deputy, and the post carried automatic placement on the board. The rule has never been rescinded. It's all there in beautiful calligraphy!'

'You might have told me!'

'An inducement in case I needed it!' he laughed. 'First law: look at the rules and regulations! If you don't like them change them, otherwise remember them. They've been formulated by the people in power and are usually designed to keep them there!'

'If it means I have to vote with you I can't accept, Cameron. I don't go along with your chicken-yard ideology; I believe in shared input.'

'That's something I can live with, Catriona. As far as I'm concerned you've already proved yourself. The only thing I'm sorry about is our inability to come up with some investment where the block could be left unmilled and yet pay its own way.'

'If you think of it please let me know!'

They were joined by the R and D section head, and Catriona outlined her suggestion. As the staff member left Cameron checked his appointment diary. 'I think I should buy you lunch! But I've only forty minutes.'

'Can I use the lift?'

He laughed and took her arm, steering her towards the foyer. Ten minutes later they were eating salad in a nearby restaurant. Catriona found the light meal with Cameron enjoyable, and she wondered if he was making an effort to get their relationship on to a comfortable work level. While they were having a drink he mentioned Rory. Catriona sighed, her dark eyebrows drawing closer as she thought about her brother.

'He went for treatment here but he's finding it difficult. And now I have to tell him about my promotion. It could hurt him.'

'Would you like me to tell him? You know I care. I could visit him tonight.'

'No, Cameron, but thank you. I'll see him this afternoon. Hopefully he will have a clearer idea of what he wants.'

'He's always realised you were flying to the top.'

She made an attempt to lighten the mood. 'You're not frightened I'll try to knock you off your perch?'

His face crinkled, his eyes gleaming. 'Not a chance—you're far too soft-hearted! You'll marry and have teenagers to worry about by the time you've gained experience to challenge me!' He glanced at his watch, forestalling her reply. 'I'll have to leave while I still can! Catriona, if you have any problems just ring me, check? I'm looking forward to your joining me.' He had the grace to laugh. 'Or, at least, working together.'

As he walked away she silently conceded that the morning had turned out better than she could have hoped; Cameron had been an understanding companion and she had enjoyed discussing work with him. Her parents, in particular her father, would be pleased with her new position. Sir James had been too shocked to say much the previous night, but plainly he was unhappy over her decision to sell the major part of her shareholding in order to buy the block. She wondered what Rory would think of her news; at least it would distract him from his own problems!

The afternoon would not be easy!

It was late when she let herself into the apartment in Wellington. The light on the phone machine winked at her like a red eye with a nervous tic, and she dumped her bags and picked up her pad almost simultaneously to annotate the list of calls waiting for her. There was not one from Cameron.

He had told her all that was necessary, so why did she feel disappointed? Had she some notion that he would have rung because he cared? He was anxious about Rory, he had respect for her parents, but just what did he feel about her? Aside from the obvious male-female attraction? Was there any hope of a sincere, loving relationship?

Slumped in a chair, tired and miserable, she regarded the list. Apart from calls from friends, there were two business calls, one from her Wellington boss, telling her he had scheduled an interview for nine-thirty the following day. She wrote it into her diary and then began unpacking her travel bag. At least once she was in Christchurch she would not be flying between the islands like an ever-migrating seagull!

The window drew her, and she stood looking out at the black harbour basin, travelling lights marking the roads, stars from homes on the hillsides and the towers of light of the commercial centre. The harbour view she would miss when she went to Christchurch. Idly she wondered where Cameron lived. Did he have a sea view? Or a river view? Remembering Bush Cabin with its magnificent outlook of forest, lake and mountains, she decided there would be little time to enjoy it. She had sent a radio message to the guide, telling him the block was to stay intact, but she had said nothing of her ownership or the details. The longer the subject could be kept confidential the better; she didn't want to rock the company's shares on the stock-market. Her father had surprised her with his mellow acceptance; his time spent learning counselling skills had reduced his abrasive wit to gentle comedy, but it was distress over Rory which had broken his anger. Catriona pushed back a few drooping curls from her forehead. Rory was having great difficulty in coping at the treatment centre. To walk away when she longed to comfort him and take him home had been hard. She had wanted to run to Cameron and blub like a baby... instead she had remembered his past and sought comfort with her parents, only to find she was the one supporting them. Again she had found herself wishing for Cameron, but she could not hurt him with their anger and grief.

Eyes grave, she moved away from the window and walked to the bedroom. If she was to keep ahead of the events happening around her sleep was essential. So it was all the more irritating when, in bed, thoughts of Cameron kept zapping in with the speed and precision of surgical laser beams.

'You want a week off? Now? Catriona, you only started work with me a month ago!' Cameron raised an eyebrow. 'Explain!'

'It's Rory! He's due to finish his treatment in a couple of days but he's not ready. I'm very worried about him. I know my taking a week off is going to mean re-arranging our schedules, but if I work late and start earlier...'

'You wouldn't ask if it wasn't necessary.' Cameron was gentle. 'But, Catriona, where will you take him? Even if you stand guard night and day for a week, what happens after that?'

'I don't know. I'm hoping that a few days away from temptation at Oranga will help. Rory said he'd like to see it. We'd need your permission...'

'Oranga! Of course. The healing place!' Cameron's hazel eyes were reflective. 'No temptation there. It just might work.' He pushed the papers he had been studying aside. 'Someone has to speak to the guide and tell him of the sale. I think you'd be the ideal person. So you won't need to take holiday leave and you can use the company plane and chopper. While you're there you can do an inventory of Bush Cabin. The prospective owner might require it!'

'You know, sometimes I could kiss you!'

'Don't let me stop you!' he laughed, but the moment passed as his secretary re-entered the room.

'I'll bring you back some smoked trout instead!'

The conversation with Cameron, more than a week earlier, came back with clarity when she saw the thin wisp of smoke rise from the smoke-house. The fishing had been excellent; her smile widened as she envisaged Cameron's delight at the boxful she had planned. She missed Cameron; the week apart had convinced her that the love she felt for him was no morning mist which would burn away in the heat of the sun.

Oranga was working its magic on Rory too, helping him to stand tall again. It had been fortunate that the guide understood; in fact, Catriona was aware that the guide's own 'been there, conquering that, one day at a time' philosophy was a part of the reason why Rory was reacting so well. But he needed more time. At Oranga she had realised how much he had been damaged. She was tempted to radio the helicopter to postpone their pick-up for another week. Cameron would be understanding but there was already a delay of a week in her scheduling. A further week would cause problems and it would rebound on to Cameron. And would another week be long enough to help Rory? Shouldn't she be realistic and ask for a month?

But hadn't there been enough ill-informed comment over her appointment without giving the media a tray of knives to throw at the family? She pulled a lugubrious face, remembering a withering comment in a well-known gossip column.

Remember Daddy's girl? Who could forget the well-known beauty? Certainly not a multi-married Wellingtonian! But he's out of the running. Daddy

might not have bought his little girl a bow-wow but
he has done his best to buy her a managing director!
And surprise, surprise! Daddy's girl has just been
appointed deputy! Be ready for the wedding of the
year, folks!

Catriona frowned at the memory. If only love were
so simple!

There had been no time to fret about gossip; working
with Cameron was a learning experience, and his intuitive
hunches left her stunned. It was a new experience to work
for someone who appreciated her ideas without her
having to think of tactful ways to recommend change.
Several times he had overruled her, but only after
studying her suggestions and then discussing the alternative strategy. Her confidence in her own decision-making
was encouraged and she enjoyed the post-mortems on
the day's activities almost as much as Cameron did. The
reorganisation dovetailed with proposals for future
growth areas and that, too, led to discussions with Sir
James and other senior staff. But there was more than
hard work involved.

Each day her smile woke with the dawn, and when
Cameron joined her in the office happiness bubbled like
a spring threatening to wash her away with joy.
Cameron's manner and careful avoidance of any personal contact meant that their relationship was kept on
a friendly business plateau. After the gossip columnist's
paragraph Catriona had even given up teasing him about
marriage. On occasions she had thought he was about
to touch her hair or make a personal comment, but each
time he had moved to his desk or to the computer, leaving
her to wonder if she had imagined it. As she had decided
to concentrate on her work and lambast any tendency

to lasciviousness it was almost with pique and certain humour that she viewed herself in the mirror. For once her looks seemed to have little attraction!

Alarm calls of birds broke into her thoughts, and she looked around, appreciating the soft, muted pink-hued tones of the sky and the darkening sweep of the lake. Rory was walking towards her.

'Pusscat, I've been thinking...' Rory's teeth gleamed white '... would you leave me here a while? I don't want to go back just yet. In fact, I think I might stay for a month or so.'

'Stay here?' It was such an obvious solution that she felt almost guilty. 'You won't get bored?'

'Bored! Here? There's so much to do!'

'What about the guide? He might not——'

'He was the one who suggested it. We get on well together. He's promised to take me climbing in the mountains. I'll need a few more clothes, but my allowance should pay for the chopper to bring in some gear... if you'll pack it up for me.'

His whimsical smile still charmed. 'Of course. Give me a list.' Standing, she began to fold the rug. A faint piping whistle stopped her.

'Kiwis!' Rory commented. 'The guide told me that there was a family of them back by the corner, but a wild cat killed the chick.'

'No!' Upset, Catriona remembered watching the little bird with Cameron. Hitching her rug into place like a cape, she followed Rory along the track, pausing at the abandoned nest. 'I wish I'd known of the danger before. But what could we have done?'

'If you're serious set up a trapping programme around the lake. There are stoats, rats, feral cats and, of course, the possums; because they're not native there are no predators. The fur trade used to keep the possums in check, but since the anti-fur lobby there's little demand, so the population is exploding. They eat the tender growing tips, and where the shrubs and trees are constantly gnawed they cannot re-grow. In places the blighters are killing the bush.'

'Should I wear a possum coat with a button saying "Save the bush"?' she teased. 'You sound like an evangelist.'

'When I grow sphagnum moss instead of hair get me out of here!' he grinned. 'You ought to talk! You gave up your inheritance for this particular patch. Some justice in that—the bush has been good to past Macarthurs! But you'll have to take some action to protect it!'

'All right, how much?'

'We'd need specialised equipment...but the guide and I could probably handle quite a lot of it...a chopper and a pilot... You could have the rest of my allowance, if that would help.'

Catriona looked at her brother, realising he had made an important breakthrough. He was once again producing ideas and suggesting work he was capable of handling.

She leaned over and hugged him. 'I'm not broke yet! I'll talk to the conservation experts at the office, maybe fly in a couple to help. We'll have to get permission from Cameron, but it will be straightforward. Dad and Mum might have some ideas, too. They plan to come soon.'

'Can you hold them off, Catriona, please? I need a little more time.' Rory's face was sober, his stance shaken. 'When I see them next I don't want to feel so bad.'

Stunned by his fragility, she nodded, too tight with emotion to speak; instead she linked her arm through her brother's and together they walked back to Bush Cabin.

'Catriona? What's the matter?' Cameron, carrying an armful of papers, entered the boardroom, catching her in a pensive mood.

'I was just thinking about Mum and Dad and their visit to Rory. They were so anxious when they left. It's been almost three months since they saw him. They're due back tonight—Dad doesn't want to risk missing another board meeting.' She made an effort to smile. 'I'm also wondering what they'll say about my valley. I feel a little like a new mother showing her infant.'

'I'm sorry I couldn't release you this time to go with them.'

'Too much work to be checked before tomorrow's meeting, I know. But you have let me have the extra Monday off several times to fly over and see Rory, and I'm grateful. You're a good boss, Cameron McDougall!'

'I picked a deputy with excellent judgement!' Laughing, he sent her a file by sliding it along the highly polished surface of the table. 'The courier just dropped these figures in—we'll need to go over them. Have you time?'

'Yes, I realised they were late and asked the chauffeur to meet Mum and Dad at the airport. They'll guess where I am.'

'Thank you. I appreciate it.' He glanced around the room. 'You arranged for the flowers? Nice touch. And the timber and hydro-power display is appropriate too. Perhaps, next time, you could set up a display on the coppicing trials. The results should please everyone;

which reminds me, did you take the reports for the Wellington office?'

'Guilty!' Catriona went to her office and returned with the file.

'Don't tell me! You just wanted to check on the Hemingway complex!'

'It finished ahead of time!'

'As though you didn't know!' His expression was good humoured.

'Tell me, Catriona, how much did the extra liaison cost?'

'All here.' She selected a sheet. 'Sixth column.'

He studied it, murmuring as his fingers followed the graph. 'A daily print-out. All materials delivered are put on computer and, reading the blueprints, it equates the men and work to be done and sections complete on site. Anything missing can be spotted. Simple but effective.' He replaced the sheet and looked up at her. 'I've not seen this programme before; where did it come from?'

Catriona made a mock bow. 'It took me hours to work out, but we needed it. I'd just managed to ease out the bugs when you insisted I give up control of the project. It's one of the reasons why I was so furious with you!'

'You should have explained. I thought it was a cover to see Ben Hamilton.'

'That doesn't deserve an answer.'

'A scratch from a tiger?' He flipped the file back into order. 'Can I borrow the programme? I'd like to show it to a friend who runs a computer company. This could be a money-spinner for you; it could have so many uses...'

'Of course.' Catriona hid her feelings. While working together their friendship had grown, but for Catriona the days were bitter-sweet. With Cameron she could discuss anything and everything—politics, religion, families, Rory's problems, conservation and, of course, work. Frequently they played tennis against or with each other, many times they had shared meals, and Cameron had even asked her to act as his hostess, but their relationship never veered towards the sexual. It seemed that Cameron had made his decision and temptation was ignored with monastic determination. To Catriona it was proving harder to bear every day. She felt as if she wore a sign saying, 'Look, but don't touch'.

Glancing out of the boardroom window, she saw the roof garden with its goldfish pool and waterlilies. Her feelings were like the plants, serene on the surface but with a tangle of need and frustration deeply rooted, hidden from view.

'Would you bring me the programme the day after the board meeting? I won't have time to action it before then.'

She could hear the faint scratch of his hand and ballpoint on paper as he diarised it.

'Anything else I should know about?'

She wanted to turn around and abuse him for insensitivity. How could an intelligent man be so stupid? What would happen if she told him she was in love with him? That working with him, seeing him several times a day, was a form of sophisticated torture?

'Can we...?' she began, then changed her mind. 'It doesn't matter.'

'You wanted to tell me something?'

Hadn't she decided that she wanted a permanent relationship, love and marriage, a home and a family, not an affair? And wasn't Cameron the man who made her heart sing? Wasn't he worth a little patience? Her lips twitched self-mockingly; she could have coped with a little patience, a little understanding, but not the daily devastation of his lack of interest. How much more could she take?

CHAPTER TEN

'CATRIONA, what were you going to say?'

Desire had stampeded her into a blind corner, and momentarily she was caught, unable to think of an appropriate question. She wished Cameron would touch her, hold her, kiss her. She wanted him. A curl flicked forward on to her face and she slapped it back, savage with herself, her principles. Under control, she looked to him. 'It wasn't anything important.' She saw his look of disbelief and hastily added, 'To the company.'

'But important for you, Catriona?'

'Yes. No! I mean...' Aware that he was looking at her, she tried for calm, but the tender sensuality in his glance set her heart beating faster. She turned away to the window to hide her inner agitation. The sounds of his soft footfalls as he walked towards her seemed amplified. She tensed as his hands began removing the clips from her hair.

'What are you doing?' Her voice was a whisper.

'Giving in to temptation,' he murmured, his mouth an inch from her ear. 'Your hair—every day you have it clipped back into place, and every day I sit in that damned chair swearing that I won't touch you... and every night after you leave I visualise you, I imagine I'm pulling out the last clip...' He held it up, forcing her to see it, then placed it on the window-ledge. 'Your hair, so silky and smooth on my fingers... caressing you...' He traced the line of her scalp with his fourth finger, then lifted the weight of the curls from her left ear, exposing its delicate pink whorls. Bending his mouth to it, he breathed on it with exquisite skill, and as the erotic fires danced she felt his hands on her hips, his fingers pressing on her abdomen, his thumbs describing circles of sensation.

'Don't!' The sound was a moan of protest. She couldn't withstand his touch, her body shivering, spasms of sensuality rippling through her body.

'Catriona...' Her name was a yearning whisper of the wind.

She felt him release her hips; then he touched the side of her face, stroking the contours around her eyes, the angle of her bones, until he cupped her chin with his fingers. It was a long physical ache waiting for his kiss. Moving with him, she felt her own melting reaction to his sensuality, her lips soft and full under his quickening passion.

'You are all woman,' his voice was rough with emotion, 'so beautiful, so vibrant.' His fingers lifted her hair, and again his mouth covered hers, kissing her so deeply that she was weightless, her consciousness soaring with his to the skies.

Reality was his gentleness as he feather-kissed her back to earth. She was content to let him hold her, aware of the new threshold they had reached, unsure of anything except her love and fierce need.

Resting against Cameron, she could hear the noisy pounding of his heart and the swift intakes of breath, smell the subtle scents of classic aftershave intermixed with fresh, warm male musk and clean, healthy skin. He moved fractionally, steadying her, and she let her hand slip back into position, curving at the line of his hip and spine. She could feel the vertebrae and the hard musculature of his back under the slight knobbly texture of his shirt and the ridge of his leather belt.

'We'll go back to my place.' The sound was a bass resonance in her ear.

Temptation lured her with her own desires and the prospect of the joy she would know with Cameron. Reality told her nothing had changed since their first encounter. He wanted her physically, but that was all; he didn't love her, he didn't want to commit himself to her. Yet she so desperately wanted to love him; had ached for his touch, for his special smile, to know his tenderness.

'Catriona, I've been waiting for some sign from you, my sweet, that you had changed your mind about marriage. You were going to ask if we could make love?'

Knowing how skilled he was at reading her expressions, she kept her eyes on his roughly pulled-down tie and open shirt button and the throb of the pulse in his neck. 'Is that what you thought?' She leaned forward a fraction, burying her nose and lips against his skin, kissing him, each time moving higher until, standing on tiptoe, she reached his mouth. 'You taught me to negotiate from a strong position, not to play all my trumps in one hand.' Her voice was husky and almost breathless.

'Catriona, you don't know how difficult you're making this.'

'Don't blame me!' she retorted.

He looked down at her through darkened eyes. 'Heaven help me, Catriona, I've wanted you since the first moment I saw you. If only you weren't so stupidly stubborn...'

'Pigheaded?' Catriona offered. She saw his lips move in wry appreciation.

'Never pigheaded!' He was smiling, his forest eyes tender. 'All right! I give up. A businessman learns to adapt to changing circumstance or he goes under. He also learns that if he wants the best he has to be prepared to pay the price. Your price was love and marriage, wasn't it?'

His capitulation stunned her.

'You are meant to say yes,' he prompted.

'Was that a proposal? It didn't sound very romantic.'

'You want hearts and flowers as well?'

'Of course!' Through deep-fringed eyelashes she looked up at him.

'You're hard to please!' He glanced around the room and strode to the floral arrangement sitting elegantly on a stand. Plucking a single pale pink rosebud, he stood for a few seconds, then moved to the display of timber. Pausing in front of it, he selected one piece then returned in triumph. 'A rose, the symbol of beauty and love, and this...' he handed her the solid piece of four-by-four timber '...totara, heart of the forest. It will stand the weathering of storms and centuries. Like my love for you, it has grown slowly, but strong.' He leaned forward and kissed her chastely. 'Satisfied?'

'Not yet.' She had the grace to blush.

'I know the feeling,' he muttered. 'You couldn't know how much I've thought about you, watched you, wanted you.'

'It wasn't at all obvious! In your eyes, I'd decided, my attraction was on a level with the computer: good memory, input and output, and user-friendly. Only I had the advantage I could share meals, talk and play tennis.'

'I didn't want to admit I'd fallen in love with you. I tried going out with several other women. It was a comic disaster. I'd be making excuses before we left the cocktail bar.' He was laughing at himself. 'Either I had to face celibacy or surrender and ask you to marry me.'

'Your choice was rather limited.'

'Yes, but yours wasn't. At the stage when you first proposed marriage it was a joke. You could have had any man you wanted. And I felt rage every time you smiled at one!'

'Your faint Scots accent when you get emotional does wicked things to me!'

'Remind me to keep a firm hold on you when we visit Scotland!'

'We'll take the children there to visit their grand-father.' She chuckled at the expression on his face. 'I told you I was greedy! I want the whole loving family nesting routine. You do like children—I've seen you with them often enough in the staff lounge. A month ago at the staff picnic they thought you were a combination of Superman and Batman. Of course, ours will be far more level-headed... Am I going too fast for you?' Her smile was of beatific innocence. 'In negotiating set out the parameters.' She was mocking him with his own lecture.

He acknowledged the thrust with the laughter lines forming around his eyes. 'You always surprise and delight me, Catriona!'

Lacing her arms around his broad back, she snuggled close to him. 'I love you so much, Cameron! I feel like champagne that's just had the cork pulled, all fizz and bubbles.' She lifted her face. 'I've been so afraid, so scared that you would never love me.'

His mouth touched hers. 'I thought I was unable to love; I was afraid to commit myself, afraid of responsibility for another person. When Diane died I felt so much guilt as well as pain. Over the years I hid the wounds of emotion under bandages of work. At the cabin it was a shock to find the bandages had fallen away, leaving healed scars. I began to care about you, but I'd been numbed for so long that I had difficulty in admitting my own emotions.' He paused and, bending his head, touched the hollow of her throat with his lips. 'You made me feel like an uncertain schoolboy again. I was longing to kiss you, to caress you and make love to you, but each time I asked you out for a meal or to act as hostess for me I became afraid.' He moved slightly to kiss the delicate shadows of her eyelids. 'I didn't want to risk loving you. To love means to trust. I couldn't.'

'What made you change your mind?' Close against him, she felt his feather-light kiss on her shoulder.

'Watching you, knowing you. The little things.'

Glancing up, she smiled at him, her lips curving as she waited for his explanation. She wanted to hear what had pleased him, intrigued or tempted him.

He touched her eyelids and her mouth with his fourth finger. 'Your smile; I love the way it dances from your eyes to your lips; you have the most beautiful eyes I've ever seen, and when you smile it lights up the stars.' He reached for her left hand and kissed her index finger. 'The habit you have of tapping this finger on your desk pad if you think someone is wasting your time.' His brief kiss stopped her moue. 'The fact that when you say you'll do something by a certain time it will be ready then; the way you won't stand fools, but if you think there's an injustice or error you'll fight me on it . . .' She frowned, but Cameron smiled. He kissed the centre spot between her eyebrows. 'You'll get wrinkle lines just there.' His regard was tender as he smoothed out the line and continued the upward motion to her scalp, where he began to stroke her hair as though unable to resist it. 'Your hair, a constant torment to me... so shiny and dark against your flawless skin. Your gracefulness, the way you move, so unconsciously sensuous. I like watching you, talking to you. When I was away from you I missed and wanted you like a man in the desert wants water! Need I say more?'

'Yes, please.' Her eyes were misty blue. 'It's a litany of love, and I think I'll ask you to repeat it every morning in bed.'

'You see,' he laughed, 'that's something else I like about you—your humour! I enjoy myself when I'm with you! We're alike in a lot of ways,' his teeth sparkled white as he grinned, 'except you have the sexier legs! And you know it... sitting across from me, all innocence and attention, and then you'll cross your legs, revealing the prettiest lace slip, and your right foot will arch up and down! My whole concentration is diverted! Do you know how much time I've spent thinking about sex with you?'

'Isn't there a proverb saying it is better to travel than to arrive?' She opened her blue eyes very wide.

'Whoever said that wasn't driving into frustration city,' he murmured.

She reached up her hands to smooth back the black hair fallen on to his forehead. The gesture was one she had longed to make and, looking into his eyes, she saw his pleasure in her touch. She felt almost shy when, reaching for her left hand, he kissed each finger in turn, then the palm, then the inside of her wrist.

'Remember our first walk?' She waited for his smile. 'When we discussed marriage and I told you I'd never marry you, I'd always be worried that you made love to my shares, not to me?'

'And I dared to tell you that you'd have to learn to trust!'

Her smile flashed sapphire-blue happiness. 'We've both learnt to trust each other. And my shares are not the reason you're marrying me! In forty-eight hours I will only have a small holding. In fact,' she kissed him fleetingly and fluttered her eyelashes provocatively, 'I could be accused of gold-digging!'

He kissed her eyelashes to still them. 'Ah! But you will have a house by one of the best fishing spots in the world! Didn't you say that could be a lure?' His mouth was hovering above hers like a bee above a honeysuckle flower. 'Besides, there are other attractions...'

The telephone's ringing broke them apart. Both stared at it as if it might develop a Medusa head. It was Cameron who picked it up, but he handed it to her.

'Pusscat? Mum and Dad love the valley! I flew back with them. But here's Mum—she's the one with the great idea!' Rory was off the line before she could speak. Wanting to share with Cameron, Catriona pushed the speaker button and laid the phone down.

'I think we should buy Oranga for the foundation,' her mother announced. 'We've been looking for a site for an addiction centre and also for a site for an adventure holiday camp. There is room for both and more!' She paused. 'It's so beautiful! But here's your father.'

'Catriona? There are problems, of course,' Sir James began. 'For a start, it's twice as big as we need, and more than twice the price that the foundation wants to pay. As your father, I don't think it is fair to ask you to sell half the area. But, wearing my hat as president of the foundation, I would like you to consider such a sale. Before you reply think about it. As it stands, Oranga has the potential for resale as a millable proposition. To cut it in half would ruin it for milling in the future, as it would then become too small.'

Catriona looked at Cameron.

'Your decision, darling,' he said softly.

She mentally sifted her ideas. 'I don't need time. I'll keep the Bush Cabin half and sell the foundation the other side. Dad, I bought it to prevent milling; I was prepared to write off my investment. If I sell there would be a condition attached to the title prohibiting milling, apart from sufficient area to set up buildings, equipment and a helipad.'

'We'd better meet tonight and discuss it.' Sir James paused. 'Do you know where Cameron is? We'll have to tell him as your share deal with the electricity company and the new subsidiary will be affected. He must re-negotiate, using half your holding and the foundation shares instead.'

'I've been listening, Sir James. It should be no problem. I'd like to welcome Rory home, too.'

'I'll pass it on. Now can you both come over? It's short notice, but we haven't a great deal of time.'

'We'll be with you in minutes.' Cameron switched off the phone. He let his hand rest on Catriona's shoulder and his thumb stroked the side of her neck in a nerve-tingling, erotic gesture. 'It looks as if I'll be marrying a millionairess, after all.'

Catriona stiffened, wondering if she had heard a note of regret in his comment. 'Do you mind?'

'In my eyes you are the woman with everything; a few millions are going to make little difference.' His lips were convincing, his hands instantly reassuring in their hold. 'We should have thought of Oranga for the foundation earlier; it was sitting under our noses and we didn't see it!'

Catriona nodded and moved to her office suite to collect her briefcase and coat. Cameron helped her to slip on her coat.

'Did you walk this morning, my Catriona?'

She loved the tender way he said her name. 'Walked! You beat me at tennis last week so I decided I'd better watch my fitness! It's a shame we can't walk home now...'

'There'll be plenty of time for walks in the moonlight in future.' He kissed her as the lift carried them down to the basement. When they were driving towards the house he was silent, leaving her time to consider her plans. Just before they pulled up she remembered to refresh her light make-up—she didn't want a lack of lipstick to be noticed.

'You are beautiful,' Cameron told her as he accompanied her to the front door. His tender look gave her joy, but before she could reply the door opened and Rory bounded down the steps.

'Isn't it great news?' He hugged Catriona, whirling her around, finally depositing her back beside Cameron.

'Rory, you look so healthy—I hope you're not after a fight!'

Cameron held out his hand. 'Am I forgiven for firing you?'

Catriona held her breath. The two men she loved had to be friends.

Rory gave his familiar golden smile. 'Guess I made life a bit of a hassle in the office. Sorry, Cameron. I owe you one!'

'Learning your weaknesses, you've found your own strengths?'

'The counselling and the spiritual dimension really helped. I don't think I could have got through without it. Walking in the bush and climbing mountains has taught me things about myself. I know what I want to do with my life now.' He paused for stage effect, using the wide-open door as a prop. 'This will surprise both of you! I've re-enrolled at university, extramurally through Massey. I'm doing subjects relating to psychology, social work and conservation.'

'Rory, I'm so pleased!' Catriona, remembering the shadow-eyed, shambling wreck she had taken to Oranga, felt the tears of joy.

'Careful, Sis, you'll smudge your mascara!'

'Isn't it wonderful?' Their parents met them in the foyer and their attitude, too, showed the relief of the pain they had felt.

Rory linked arms with them. 'When I finish my degree I may get my last few points of my commerce degree, but then I'm going to apply for a job at the foundation. With qualifications, I figure I'll be quite useful; I've learnt a lot about myself and addiction, so, hopefully, I can give others some help. And I may be able to assist on the sports side. The valley could be a great spot for teaching and training in sailing, swimming, tennis, fishing, wind-surfing, tramping and mountain climbing. There's even a basin for a ski-field!'

'You want to live there?' It was Cameron who put the question.

'Why not? It's a fantastic place. I want to do something useful for others, and there I can. I'll get my pilot's licence and then my chopper ticket. With that, isolation is no problem!'

'What about Macarthur's?' Again it was Cameron who asked the question.

'There's no need for me to work there. You can handle it. You and Catriona and the rest of the board. Perhaps at some future time I'll consider a directorship, but I can't guarantee it. I have a feeling that the foundation will take over my life.' He pulled a comic face. 'Enough of me—let's get on with the project!'

Still talking, he led the way to the resource-room, where full-size maps of the block were spread over the large table. 'As I see it, the cost of all the land would deplete the foundation's funds. The principle has been to set aside sufficient capital from the government grant and the Macarthur gift to supply an annual cash-flow. We've worked out exactly how much we can afford to pay for land and buildings. This site is marvellous, but we really don't need such a vast acreage. Pusscat has agreed to sell half, which brings the proposition to a figure two hundred thousand above the amount set aside for the sites. That money is part of the development and site planning...' He looked expectantly at Catriona.

She felt like hugging Rory, she was so delighted with her brother's sudden business perspicacity, and she couldn't resist teasing him. 'Always presuming I was going to sell at the same price I paid. Macarthurs always try for a profit!'

Rory was equal to her challenge. He pulled a woebegone face. 'I would like the foundation to be able to buy half, but there are other less expensive sites. Not as good . . .'

'All right, I'll drop my price.' Catriona was too happy to continue the charade. 'I'll settle for five hundred thousand less—with two conditions. Once the building is finished I want a guarantee that no noisy gear, which could disturb the peace for everyone else, will be used. And the foundation gives me a contract subject to governmental approval within twelve hours. It will save me quite a lot if I can avoid brokerage fees for half my shareholding.'

'If you are certain, Catriona.' Sir James nodded. 'I suggest you write down the conditions you want. I've called the family solicitor and the foundation board members.'

'It might pay you to insert a clause on conservation care,' Cameron suggested. 'In a hundred years' time the foundation, or its representatives, would still be guardians.'

Catriona flashed him a grateful glance before she sat down to a computer keyboard and began screening her words.

Twenty hours later Catriona leaned by the window in her office. Tiredness showed in her stance, her shoulders sagging against the frame. She knew she should be playing hostess to the directors but she needed a few minutes' respite. Hearing the door open, she made an effort to straighten but her muscles seemed to lack coordination. Yet when she saw Cameron she felt her energy return, and ran joyfully to his arms.

'Congratulations, my darling!' His kiss was brief. 'The whole deal from the board to the electricity company handled like silk.' He kissed her again, lingering on her mouth. 'But you wish I hadn't been forced to announce our engagement in the middle of a board meeting? I'm sorry, but I had to declare my interest and step down from the chair over the question.'

'You had no choice! Although I would have preferred to tell Mum and Dad and Rory on their own. Did you see Dad's expression?' She chuckled, remembering. 'Just as well he has his own teeth, his jaw dropped so far!'

Smiling, Cameron wrapped her in his arms. 'Mmm. They deserve full marks for a speedy recovery, though!' He bent his head to kiss her gently, his hands caressing her. 'Come on, we'd better go and face everyone. You were the one who persuaded me the dinner for the directors was better than a lunch!'

'I think we'll find it will have been turned into an engagement party!'

His lips were on hers and she raised her head to deepen the kiss. Passion flared as the moment lengthened, threatening to overwhelm them until Catriona felt Cameron ease his hold.

'I love you, Catriona.' He murmured the words between quick touches of his tongue and lips. 'When are we going to have some time alone?'

'Moot point! Tomorrow you have the forestry regional meeting in Nelson, and before you return I fly off to the Sydney office for a week. It will be three weeks before we have a few days clear.'

'We will have to reorganise our schedules together. Otherwise we are going to have a very frustrating relationship.'

'I'm glad you see the problem. Dad was a workaholic; when we were small we hardly saw him. I don't want to repeat the pattern. It wasn't so bad for me, because I used to have Grandad.'

'It's a natural concern. Other priorities take precedence so often.' He looked at her and smiled. 'Management techniques?'

'Recognise the potential problem, suggest ways to avoid same.'

'If we admit that our supposed free time in the evenings and weekends is often interrupted by business, travel, friends and family then we can see the need to plan time to ourselves.' He paused. 'Time we can diarise... for a start, let's try four hours. Some weeks we might tie it on to either end of a weekend to give us a long break, or we could take a morning off together after one of us has been away. We could do things together, take a couple of long lunch-hours, walk on the beach, I could beat you at tennis...'

'Make love...' Her blue eyes sparkled.

'A distinct possibility!' He kissed the top of her head. 'Where's your diary? I want to write in it now.'

Surprised, she picked it up from her desk and handed it to him. He took his ballpoint from a top pocket and wrote two words, one on each page, and scored a follow-on line through the weekend and the Monday.

'Wedding, honeymoon,' she read. 'But that's only three weeks away!'

He ran his finger along the inside of her left arm from the wrist to the elbow, then kissed the palm of her hand.

'We know our own minds. Besides, any longer and you won't be able to keep your hands off me,' he teased, his eyes full of laughter and light, 'but, seeing this is an equal partnership, you're allowed to pick the time of day and place.'

'I should pick the South Pole so that there is only one way forward! But the logistics would be a little much to arrange in three weeks, even with the sun shining twenty-four hours a day! How about our garden at home? And in the afternoon? The time will depend on our minister.'

She felt his hands caress her back and shoulders and she reached forward and kissed him. 'There'll hardly be time for a honeymoon.'

'Yes, there will.' His words were definite. 'I don't care if our secretaries have to postpone two dozen meetings. My wife will come before any business. I've learnt that lesson.'

She looked at him and he met her enquiry.

'Don't worry, Catriona, my darling. I know you. Just now you are hesitating, thinking about Diane.'

'Yes.'

'I'm not denying the love I felt for Diane. I never will. I could say then I was a boy, now I am a man, but that would be demeaning to you, to Diane and to myself. The experiences that I've been through have changed me. So there can be no comparisons. I love you, my Catriona. Without you I would have gone on spending my time in business, because that would have been better than nothing. But with you I have everything. It is that simple.' He traced her face with his fingertips. 'Catriona...'

She basked in his love like a cat in front of a log fire, relaxed, happy and sure of her place. 'Mr Chairman, as your deputy should I remind you there are a lot of others waiting for us?'

'Possibly, but they can wait a few minutes longer. I have to ask my deputy if she would be able to help me track down the owner of a certain romantic bush cabin where my bride might like to spend our honeymoon.'

'Cameron, of course!' She smiled at him, her eyes misty blue. 'The heart of the forest, the perfect place, Oranga!'

'With you, my love, any place becomes perfect.'

Catriona saw in the shining happiness of his eyes the only way to answer him.

HARLEQUIN
Romance®

and WEDDINGS go together—
especially in June!
So don't miss next month's title in

THE BRIDAL COLLECTION

LOVE YOUR ENEMY
by Ellen James

THE BRIDE led the anti-Jarrett forces.
THE GROOM was Jarrett!
THE WEDDING? An Attraction of Opposites!

Available this month in
THE BRIDAL COLLECTION

THE MAN YOU'LL MARRY
by Debbie Macomber
Harlequin Romance (#3196)
Wherever Harlequin books are sold.

WED-2

FREE GIFT OFFER

To receive your free gift, send us the specified number of proofs-of-purchase from any specially marked Free Gift Offer Harlequin or Silhouette book with the Free Gift Certificate properly completed, plus a check or money order (do not send cash) to cover postage and handling payable to Harlequin/Silhouette Free Gift Promotion Offer. We will send you the specified gift.

FREE GIFT CERTIFICATE

ITEM	A. GOLD TONE EARRINGS	B. GOLD TONE BRACELET	C. GOLD TONE NECKLACE
# of proofs-of-purchase required	3	6	9
Postage and Handling	$1.75	$2.25	$2.75
Check one	☐	☐	☐

Name: _____

Address: _____

City: _____ State: _____ Zip Code: _____

Mail this certificate, specified number of proofs-of-purchase and a check or money order for postage and handling to: HARLEQUIN/SILHOUETTE FREE GIFT OFFER 1992, P.O. Box 9057, Buffalo, NY 14269-9057. Requests must be received by July 31, 1992.

PLUS—Every time you submit a completed certificate with the correct number of proofs-of-purchase, you are automatically entered in our MILLION DOLLAR SWEEPSTAKES! No purchase or obligation necessary to enter. See below for alternate means of entry and how to obtain complete sweepstakes rules.

MILLION DOLLAR SWEEPSTAKES
NO PURCHASE OR OBLIGATION NECESSARY TO ENTER

To enter, hand-print (mechanical reproductions are not acceptable) your name and address on a 3" ×5" card and mail to Million Dollar Sweepstakes 6097, c/o either P.O. Box 9056, Buffalo, NY 14269-9056 or P.O. Box 621, Fort Erie, Ontario L2A 5X3. Limit: one entry per envelope. Entries must be sent via 1st-class mail. For eligibility, entries must be received no later than March 31, 1994. No liability is assumed for printing errors, lost, late or misdirected entries.

Sweepstakes is open to persons 18 years of age or older. All applicable laws and regulations apply. Sweepstakes offer void wherever prohibited by law. Prizewinners will be determined no later than May 1994. Chances of winning are determined by the number of entries distributed and received. For a copy of the Official Rules governing this sweepstakes offer, send a self-addressed, stamped envelope (WA residents need not affix return postage) to: Million Dollar Sweepstakes Rules, P.O. Box 4733, Blair, NE 68009.

✂ HR2U

ONE PROOF-OF-PURCHASE
To collect your fabulous FREE GIFT you must include the necessary FREE GIFT proofs-of-purchase with a properly completed offer certificate.

(See inside back cover for offer details)

Coming Next Month

#3199 A CINDERELLA AFFAIR Anne Beaumont
They met one stormy day in Paris—and fell in love. Their affair was brief, yet sweet and loving. It ended when Briony realized she must return to England to marry Matthew. But how can she leave Paul for a life that will have no meaning?

#3200 WILD TEMPTATION Elizabeth Duke
Bram Wild, her new boss, has a legendary reputation as a womanizer, but Mia feels sure she's immune to his wicked charms. After all, she's happy with her dependable fiancé—and why in the world would Bram be interested in her in any case...?

#3201 BRAZILIAN ENCHANTMENT Catherine George
When Kate arrives in Villa Nova to teach English, the tiny Brazilian mountain town begins to work its magic on her. The same couldn't be said of her imperious employer, Luis Vasconcelos, whose rude welcome makes Kate resolve to avoid him. But that's something that proves rather difficult.

#3202 LOVE YOUR ENEMY Ellen James
They're natural enemies. Lindy MacAllister, dedicated conservationist. She's determined to protect ''her'' colony of burrowing owls. Nick Jarrett, designer of airplanes. He's equally determined to get his new factory built, on schedule and on the selected site. When the immovable object (Lindy) meets the irresistible force (Nick)—watch out!
LOVE YOUR ENEMY is the second title in Harlequin Romance's The Bridal Collection.

#3203 RUNAWAY FROM LOVE Jessica Steele
The job offer in Thailand seems heaven-sent to Delfi. She has to get away—she's afraid she's becoming attracted to her sister's fiancé! Yet, alone in Bangkok, with Boden McLaine the only person she can turn to, Delfi wonders if she's jumped from the frying pan into the fire!

#3204 NEW LEASE ON LOVE Shannon Waverly
Nick Tanner is exactly the kind of man Chelsea wants. He's dynamic, attractive and his little daughter, Katie, is adorable. Nick even seems to be sending out the right messages... to the wrong woman!

AVAILABLE THIS MONTH:

#3193 THE WRONG KIND OF MAN
Rosemary Hammond

#3194 FOR LOVE OR POWER
Rosalie Henaghan

#3195 ROMANTIC JOURNEY
Stephanie Howard

#3196 THE MAN YOU'LL MARRY
Debbie Macomber

#3197 THE FINAL TOUCH
Betty Neels

#3198 PRINCE OF DELIGHTS
Renee Roszel

Harlequin®

JANELLE TAYLOR

Valley of Fire

OVER THE YEARS, TELEVISION HAS BROUGHT
THE LIVES AND LOVES OF MANY CHARACTERS INTO
YOUR HOMES. NOW HARLEQUIN INTRODUCES YOU
TO THE TOWN AND PEOPLE OF

One small town—twelve terrific love stories.

GREAT READING...GREAT SAVINGS...AND A FABULOUS
FREE GIFT!

Each book set in Tyler is a self-contained love story; together, the
twelve novels stitch the fabric of the community.

By collecting proofs-of-purchase found in each Tyler book, you can
receive a fabulous gift, ABSOLUTELY FREE! And use our special
Tyler coupons to save on your next TYLER book purchase.

Join us for the fourth TYLER book,
MONKEY WRENCH by Nancy Martin.

*Can elderly Rose Atkins successfully bring a new love into
granddaughter Susannah's life?*